The Internet of Things

David R J Sealey

ONE

The train whipped past the platform at a hundred miles an hour, blowing up skirts, sweeping up luggage and scattering passengers on the platform in its wake. The public address system blared its overly-polite warning much too late.

"PLEASE KEEP BACK FROM THE PLATFORM EDGE. WE HAVE AN UNSCHEDULED ARRIVAL. PLEASE KEEP BACK FROM THE PLATFORM EDGE..."

A motorbike roared out of the station house, breaking through the turnstiles and screeched to a halt on the platform. A thin man, wearing a black duster and a red helmet, sat astride the chopper's hardtail frame taking stock, gripping the high ape hanger handle bars with leather gloved hands. The rogue train had raced clear of the platform. The thin man gunned the engine and accelerated up the platform, knocking over the last passengers lucky enough to remain standing. A prone old woman muttered under her breath and made crude hand gestures after him as he disappeared into the distance. Her husband staggered to his feet, shaking his stick furiously, his cheeks a rich beetroot red.

"You goddamned animal! Young people these days! Well, I never..."

The bike tore up the concourse and leapt into the air as the platform abruptly ran out beneath it, clearing the black iron railings that marked the station boundaries by several feet and landed with a jolt on the gravel path that ran parallel along the tracks. The thin man managed to hold the back-end steady as he felt it begin to slide out from beneath him; not this time. He had business to attend to before he took that final ride out into the great beyond, bound and gagged business that was fast disappearing around a bend in the track up ahead, behind a steep embankment.

The thin man did not turn as the tracks bore left; he just held his line straight ahead as he accelerated up the embankment. The bike soared into the air, easily clearing the muddy river on the other side and fell back to earth with a nasty jolt. He steadied the bike and found himself tearing blindly through a bumpy field full of rows of tall, plump corn, the ears slapping and breaking against his helmet, obscuring his view. He concentrated on what he could hear instead as he held his course. The sound of the train bore away left, becoming fainter. He tried to tune out the rustling corn, the growl of the motorbike engine; the rhythmic chugging grew louder again somewhere up ahead. Any moment now...

He stood forward on his haunches, crouching low over the handlebars and opened the throttle as far as it would go. The chopper hurtled faster and faster and then the corn slapped no more. The thin man hit the embankment at top speed as he broke free of the field and the chopper leapt into the air once more. The train emerged around the bend beneath him, clattering along the tracks; he could hear it creaking in protest as it juddered along the track at constant high speed. It sounded as though it was shaking itself to pieces. He added to its woe as the bikes tyres bit into the thin metal, leaving two round dents behind him as he tore along the roof of the speeding train, clearing the narrow gaps between the carriages. It wasn't long before he ran out of roof.

The thin man half-jumped, half-fell backwards from the chopper as it cleared the engine cab and caught beneath the front of the train, sending up great showers of sparks as it dragged along the tracks. He wobbled on the edge of the roof as the train ground to a halt, clutching on with his gloved hands. A man wearing a blue cloth cap stuck his head out of the engine cab window beneath him. A frantic, hurried discussion took place inside.

"What the heck was that?"

"Shut up and keep going. Who told you to stop?"

"I can see a tyre down there, some metal..."

"Hey! Who told you to stop? Dan, did you tell this motherfucker to stop the train?"

"Nah boss, I didn't say a thing."

"I can't run the train with that thing stuck down there! It's a breach of health and safety regulations!"

The guy leaning out of the window must be the driver, a friendly. The barrel of a silenced pistol crept out of the window behind him and pressed lightly against the back of his head, beneath his cap.

"Just keep going Mother Theresa and I won't blow that dumb cap off your dumb head. That's right, back in the cab, there's a good boy."

The driver's head disappeared back into the cab and the engine rumbled back into life. The thin man removed his red helmet, swung it downwards as hard as he could and launched it in through the open window at a vicious pace. He heard a satisfying fleshy 'thunk' accompanied by a scream as he clambered down past the door on the opposite side of the train and peered in through the dirty window.

The man with the gun was holding a thickset man, Dan presumably, up by his lapels and screaming at the driver to open the door.

The thin man smashed his black gloved fist through the closed cab window, grabbed the boss-man's jacket collar from behind and hauled him out through the open window, knocking the pistol from his hand against the frame. It clattered down out of sight beneath the striped seats of the cab.

The boss-man's chubby face turned white as the thin man pushed his head towards the broken window, a sharp glass shard glittering just inches from his eye.

"Who...who are you?"

"Where is she?"

"What do you want? Are you a cop?"

The thin man pushed the boss-man's head further down, stopping just short of the glass puncturing his eye. He was in charge here. The boss-man whimpered like a bad puppy.

"Where is she?"

"What do you want? I've got money. Lots of money"

"Last chance Jack, where is she?"

He put more pressure on the boss-man's neck and positioned his foot against the back of his knee. With just the slightest push, the glass would make short work of his eye and, with any luck, penetrate his brain. A sudden smell of urine told him that the boss-man had had enough. His voice broke as he surrendered.

"Ok, ok, tough guy, you win. She's in the middle carriage, but she's being watched. I got four of my best guys in there. You won't get in there without one of them pulling the trigger."

"That's why you're coming with me, Jack"

"I'm not going any.."

His defiance ended mid-sentence as the bullet ripped through his jaw, tearing it from his face. Blood sprayed from his open throat like a macabre water-feature; the thin man released his grip and the boss-man's body fell by the trackside. The driver stood shaking in the cab, the pistol limp in his hands.

"I'm s-s-s-sorry. I just... I don't know what happened."

"Give me the gun please, sir."

"Yes, yes, the gun. Of course, here, please take it. Thank you."

As he handed it over, a look of doubt crossed his face.

"Are...are you a cop?

"I'm a force of nature, pal. What's your name?"

"Michael, well, Mike really."

"Well, thanks for the gun, Mike Really. It's a pleasure to meet you."

The thin man held his hand out and, as Mike moved to shake it, he leant into the cab past him and fired two rounds one-handed into the back of henchman Dan's shaven head. The good old double-tap, just to make sure; the sight of more blood sent poor Mike the driver over the edge. He curled up into a ball, sobbing, wiping his face over and over with his cap.

"Sorry about that bud, the pipes were calling. Better Danny boy than you."

"Oh god, oh god, I killed him. They're dead. I shot him..."

The thin man left him to cry it out; he felt sorry for Mike. He hadn't expected things to go all Jack Bauer while he was tucking into his cornflakes that morning; just another day. But that's all it was, just another day; someone lives, someone dies, it's all just blood under the bridge.

He clambered up onto the carriage behind the engine cab and peered in through the window; all clear. He slowly pushed open the door.

There were bodies in the seats and in the aisle, men and women in bloody business suits lying amongst scattered laptops and phones. The sad remnants of a final early morning run into the city; just Joe and Josephine Average on their way into the office. It had just been another day, but there would never be another for these poor souls. The thin man checked the gun; it was a silenced Glock, six rounds left in the clip. He stepped over the fallen and peered through the little foggy window in the connecting door. Someone was headed his way.

He quickly stood to the side of the door as it opened and an enormous Asian man stepped a long, loping pace through into the carriage, his shaven head bobbing from left to right. The thin man looked back through the open door behind him, holding his breath. Just maintain, a moment longer... There she was! The blonde, bound and gagged, sat between a fat guy in a creased suit and some weird–looking asshole in a full-face balaclava. The thin man pointed the silenced pistol at the back of the big Asian guy's thick neck, squeezed the trigger tight and stepped into the open door-frame before the body hit the floor.

The fat guy in the suit went to pull something from beneath his shoulder but took a round full in his shocked, pudgy face before he could make it. Balaclava dropped beneath the level of the seat as the door at the other end of the carriage opened and a skinny black guy carrying an assault rifle entered the fray. Moments later, he too fell where he stood, clutching at his throat. The thin man heard the blonde screaming through the cloth wadded in her mouth. Not long now, love...

The balaclava guy suddenly leapt out at him from his left, bearing a knife. He ducked and moved lithely aside as balaclava landed on his feet and swung the blade wildly in his direction. It was more machete than knife. The thin man knew what to do with an idiot like this. He rolled backwards, stood and put on his best Australian accent.

"That's not a knife."

Balaclava stood, confused a moment.

"What?"

"That's not a knife, mate"

"What's your name? Crocodile..."

The bullet took him by surprise, lifting him from his feet mid-sentence and sent him sprawling against the side of the train. The thin man towered over him as he spluttered and clawed at the air.

"Isn't that just like a ninja? Brings a knife to a gunfight."

The thin man knew the quote was inaccurate, but that was the least of his worries. When he was sure it was over, he rushed to free the blonde. He used balaclava's knife to cut her free and pulled the gag from her mouth.

"You came!"

"You know that's never been a problem for me, doll"

She looked up at him, doe-eyed.

"My hero."

He swept her up in his arms and gave her a kiss. A big wet kiss, very sloppy, not that pleasant; her tongue felt enormous. She was being a little rough to be honest, and, what was that, stubble? Something rumbled near his groin.

The thin man opened his eyes to see a cow's face mere inches from his own, its dirty stinking tongue pressing into his mouth as it leant over the stall. He leapt groggily to his feet and backed away from the bovine.

"Christ! What the hell?"

He realised there was nobody there to hear him; he was alone in the barn, just him, the stink and the cows watching him suspiciously from their enclosure. He spat and wretched as the slutty one looked coyly at him, fluttering her eyelashes. No one must know of this. He cancelled rubbed the sleep from his eyes, trying desperately to remember how he'd ended up in this compromising position.

The thin man turned and stumbled out of the barn into an empty, soggy overgrown field; his rust-bucket car was parked up by the gate, the driver's side door wide open. His phone rumbled in his pocket. He took it out as he walked, kicking up the dew, looked at the clock and groaned. There was no rest for the wicked; it was time to solve a murder.

TWO

A torrential river of tarmac piled past the smeared windows, keeping the car afloat. The storm was coming on fast, dark blue ink spreading across a paper white sky. The thin man pushed the fedora higher up onto his forehead as he checked the clock; 12:17 PM. He was late.

His foot weighed down heavily on the accelerator, pinning it to the floor beneath his black-patent Dr. Martens boot. The car's engine roared in protest as he wrestled with its gears with his prosthetic arm before he finally found the sweet spot and slammed the grating box into third. He had slowly grown used to the strange flesh-coloured lump of metal and plastic attached to his left shoulder, sometimes forgetting it was there at all.

A sign zipped past in the failing light; three miles remaining. The roadside buildings were slowly growing taller as he approached the city limits. How many windows had he driven past so far; hundreds, thousands? How many people lived their lives behind each double-glazed PVC window? It must be tens of thousands. And what were they all doing, scratching around in their cells, mouths agape, their hands down their pants, hypnotised by LCD displays? He shook his head at the thought. It made him itch.

A rhythmic whirring started up to his left; a plastic rumble that shook him from his waking daze. The neon blue screen demanded his attention again. With a sigh, he answered.

"Bruce Von Toose, Private Investigator."

"Bruce! At last, you actually pick up. You are an elusive one."

The voice was male, high and nasal. Unwelcome.

"It comes with the territory, Jack. And who might you be, my rodent-larynxed friend?"

"It's Jimmy, Jimmy Masters. Are you still coming to see me today, Mr. von Toose? I'm a very busy man; I'm in a conference call from 12:30 and then I'm back-to-back all freaking week. Time is money in my world, Mr. von Toose!"

Jimmy's register got higher as he got madder. Bruce had to think fast.

"Jimmy, if I were you, I'd quit running my mouth right about now and listen to two solid gold FACTS. Fact one; I've been delayed by circumstances beyond my control. My dear old mother has been rushed to hospital this very morning. And fact number two? I'm outside right now, trying to find a space in your shoddily equipped car park in the lunch hour rush, wasting time arguing with YOU. So, I'll be two minutes, and it's all your fault anyway. You got that, Jim-bob?"

Jimmy made a strange noise, halfway between a cough and splutter.

"Look Bruce, call me Jimmy or Mr. Masters please. I'm meeting the Itsy Bitsy Girls at one. Can't we..."

"No Jimmy, we can't. Keep the toys in the pram you big, spoilt baby, I'll be two minutes! I don't care if you're having a threesome in a teeny-weeny yellow polka-dot bikini at one, I'm coming in. Stop your damn whining."

He made the choking sound again, like he'd just swallowed his diary.

"Really now Mr. Von Toose, that is quite enough! I don't even know what the hell this is about!"

"You don't know, really, Jimmy? I'm doing you a favour here! Like I said, I need to talk to you about our mutual client, a certain Mr. Mastah Blastah. There's been a development"

Jimmy was silent for a moment. Bruce could hear the cogs whirring. Finally, he spoke.

"Get down here in the next five minutes or you can forget it, Mr. von Toose."

Jimmy hung up.

Bruce tossed the phone back onto his passenger seat, the screen illuminating crumbs and stains in the grey fabric like the great boulders and seas on the bright side of the moon. He caught a glimpse of himself in the cold light; it was not a pretty sight. His blue-tinged face highlighted his bulging pink eyes and he wore the stubble of several days. As if to match his mood, the storm finally broke and a hard rain began to fall, beating heavily against the car roof as he drove. He flicked the wipers on; you've got to love British summer time.

With one eye on the road and his prosthetic hand on the wheel, Bruce lit a cigarette and drifted back into his thoughts. Mastah Blastah was still nowhere to be found. He did have a lead. Jimmy Masters' name had come up. He was Mastah Blastah's agent, manager, and chief back-stabber by all accounts. One of the first rules of the detective game; look to see who stands to gain from the crime and you will find your man. Jimmy had a motive. That was enough.

The smoke traced a path through the spreading darkness; twisting back and forth, gently losing definition. Bruce had to deduce fact from the steadily diffusing cloud of fiction. Luckily, that was his forte. A fork of lightning pierced the bleak horizon, beyond the distant tower blocks. Jimmy was a slippery eel that needed putting in a pie. He'd sounded strung out on the phone, tired, his nerves were frayed. He would talk. They all talked, in the end.

The lights of the city approached and enveloped the car as he neared his destination, strobing across his face. He wound down the window; the bitter winter wind cut into the cockpit as he dispatched the spent smouldering butt road-wards. Blue light flashed far off in the distance. Realising his speed, Bruce eased up on the accelerator so that his speedometer matched the angry signs buzzing past and wound his window shut.

Paradise Records loomed before him; a hulking block of concrete and glass, all rubberised seals and 1970's dementia. He found a space in the near empty car park almost straight away and checked the clock on his phone as he dropped it into his jacket pocket.

It was 12:22 PM. He was late, again.

Jimmy was going to be apoplectic. Bruce imagined the owner of that stupid, ferrety voice pacing around an office, cursing his name, wishing harm upon him, calling him every name under the sun and couldn't help but laugh. This was going to be a walk in the park.

THREE

The Paradise Records lobby was awash with white marble and light, punctuated by long black leather benches and the label's logo liberally sprinkled around the joint to the point of distraction. An expensive neon-blue glass reception desk loomed out at Bruce from beneath the myriad of pucker-faced portraits and gold discs lining the white walls. Three men, all black sunglasses, puffer jackets and short, sharp haircuts, sat together across the room, talking in furious whispers and glancing over at him when they thought he wasn't looking. Bruce watched them chattering out the corner of his eye; they wouldn't have a chance.

He lit a cigarette to calm his nerve like a nervous twitch, no thought, just an instinctive, automatic reaction to quell the sudden craving. A laugh echoed out across the room from one of the guys; a crazy hyena's cackle that caught him off guard. Bruce's feet slid out from beneath him on the slick polished floor, and he pirouetted awkwardly toward the blue whale of a desk. He caught hold of the edge and steadied himself. There was nobody sat behind its lonely expanse. He caught his breath. An old-fashioned brass push bell sat awkwardly at odds with the slick modern decor. Bruce hit it, with gusto, hard and fast with his prosthetic hand. It rang out with the sound and effect of musical machine-gun. The receptionist came running.

"Sorry, excuse me sir, how can I help you?"

The woman had a severe look about her; something about the way she bustled in through the door told him she was trouble. Pale skin, a curt brown bob, red lips and black holes for eyes; she challenged him with a stare.

"There's no smoking allowed in here sir. Please extinguish your cigarette in the receptacle." She pointed out the bin. "What name is it?"

He stubbed the cigarette out on the chrome lid without breaking eye contact with the receptionist. She jutted her chin at him; asking for a response. He gave it to her at last.

"What's my name, doll? Von Toose, Private Investigator. You can call me Bruce. I have a 12…"

Her fingers flew at the keyboard as he spoke and she cut him off victoriously.

"Well, I'm afraid it is 12:27 now Mr. von Toose, I'm afraid you're late. Your appointment is over. I can try and make you an alternative meeting, tomorrow perhaps, or next week?"

She turned robotically to face the screen, a smirk dancing at the edge of her glossy lips at another small victory won in the war against tardiness. Bruce smiled; the battle had barely begun.

"Tomorrow's no good lady; you don't get it, I spoke to Jimmy, your boss, on the phone not five minutes ago. He's expecting me, I'm *special.* And if you delay our meeting just one more minute, just one, I'll call him myself and you'll be crying over the job pages in the morning. Is that what you want?"

He waved his phone at her, Jimmy's number on the screen; she didn't like it. She adjusted her headset and pressed the button on the side.

"There's A Mr. Von Toose here to see you. Mr. Masters; he seems rather impatient."

A crackling exploded from her headset and she cowered beneath the words.

"Yes, yes sir. Yes, I'll send him straight through. I must apologise…. OK."

She pointed at the double doors to her right, shaking her head. She opened her mouth to speak; Bruce beat her to it. He held up his hand.

"I'm on my way."

He turned on his heel and left her staring blankly into space.

Bruce pushed the call button; the lift doors slid aside soundlessly at his touch and he stepped inside. Masters name was written on a plate at the top of the list of floors, the only name in the company of numbers. Masters was evidently a big cheese, shame he was rotten. He hit the button and adjusted his collar and pulled his hat brim low as the lift ascended silently toward the penthouse.

Moments later, the doors opened to reveal a small waiting area; two impractical looking bright red Teletubbies-esque chairs sat either side of an indoor palm tree, beneath yet more blown-up shots of air-brushed female faces. Across the hallway lay a vast heavy black wooden door bearing a name carved into an ostentatious golden plaque. It looked as though it belonged out front on Downing Street. Jimmy sure had a keen sense of his own importance.

Bruce walked across the waiting area and, without knocking, tried the handle. It wasn't locked. His eyes darted around the lobby; no cameras. Maybe it was overconfidence, maybe it was arrogance; either way this was going to be a walk in the park.

Bruce stepped into the darkened office. Through the brass-handled, heavy door lay an even larger breed of desk, the top hewn from marble and mounted on a heavily carved ornate wooden base. Inside, the room was all subtle shades of carefully backlit green and rich mahogany, curling cigar smoke, deep crimsons and gold. A Wurlitzer jukebox sat gleaming in the corner, next to a chest high mini-bar equipped with a crystal decanter full of some high-end booze. The blinds were shut against the light of day and a classy looking art deco lamp stood in for the sun. A stern, high-backed red leather chair sat behind the desk, housing a snorting, brooding, deep-set figure with a terrible haircut. Jimmy gestured for him to take a seat. Bruce took his hat off slowly, ignoring him, avoiding eye contact. Jimmy couldn't take the awkward silence a moment longer. He looked at his watch pointedly before he spoke.

"Mr. von Toose I presume? You're late, sir!"

Jimmy's little round glasses had steamed up and his loose chin quivered as he spoke. He watched as Bruce walked back across the room and turned the heavy key in the door's lock.

"Forget about me, Jimmy. Let's talk about you. This won't take long. When did you last see Mastah Blastah? Was it around the last time you saw your own feet?"

Bruce looked Jimmy square in the eye as he approached the desk; he watched beads of sweat forming on the fat man's forehead. His prosthetic arm hissed at his side, coiling to strike; he felt like a loaded viper. Jimmy was taken aback.

"Excuse me? Do you know who I am, Mr. von Toose? I know who you are, you scumbag; my people do their homework."

Bruce leant forward.

"So, you know my name, I gave that to you on the phone brainiac. But who's to say that's my real name? Sounds kind of made-up, doesn't it? But no, you're right, the real question here is who the fuck are you, Jimmy? Really, who are you beneath that sea of gut? All I'm seeing here is talking cheeseburger."

Jimmy went on the defensive; clearly the fat boy jokes were hitting their mark.

"I'm a decent family man, Mr. von Toose, unlike yourself sir. I'm the boss of a leading record label. I go to Church every Sunday morning and play football with my kids in my gigantic, beautiful garden in the afternoon. I put six figures on the table, without fail, every single month! I'm successful, unlike yourself sir, and what's so bad about that? You're just some washed up wannabe rent-a-cop with anger management issues. You barely exist!"

The outpouring of rage had taken it out of him; he mopped at his sodden brow with an expensive cuff. Bruce lunged suddenly, grabbing Jimmy by his pricey lapels and dragging him across the desk, bringing his round, boarish face to within an inch of his own. He could taste the fat man's breath, sour on his tongue. Bruce shook him viciously.

"What did you do to Mastah Blastah?"

Jimmy's eyes bobbled around in their sockets like a stuffed toy. He reached for his desk drawer, a look of desperation on his face. Bruce drove his forehead down hard into the other mans crown and released his grip on his shirt. Jimmy flopped back onto his chair bleeding from the forehead, his mouth opening and closing like a fish out of water, his glasses broken in half. Bruce wrenched the drawer open with his prosthetic arm, almost tearing it from the desk; a small black pistol sat on top of a pile of papers. Bruce seized the gun in his good hand and pointed it at Jimmy's gut.

"What were you going to do, shoot me? Who've you been messing around with Jimmy? Start talking or I swear it's all over for you. Where did you get this piece? I wouldn't think twice about wasting a scumbag like you. You sold out your own damn client!"

Bruce held the gun up in his good hand and used his prosthetic to crush the barrel flat in front of Jimmy's fat face. The useless weapon clattered to the wooden office floor. Bruce grabbed him by the lapels again. Jimmy began to sob uncontrollably. His tears rolled down Bruce's clenched fists.

"Please, don't hurt me. I don't know anything! Mastah Blastah was just an employee..."

Bruce shook him again, harder and slapped his chubby face, a tremendous blow that caught them both by surprise. Bruce regained his composure.

"Don't lie to me Jimmy! He was more than that! He was your biggest earner, one of your first big acts. Why did you have him killed?"

Jimmy was shell-shocked; the slap had broken him. His breathing was ragged, fast and shallow; his eyes were closed. Bruce's prosthetic arm began to twitch uncontrollably. It seemed somehow to be angrier than the rest of him. Bruce slapped him again.

"TALK TO ME YOU WORTHLESS PIG! WHAT DID YOU DO TO HIM?"

Still no answer, the man was hysterical, pathetic, a blubbering wreck. Bruce brought his prosthetic metal fist to bear and buried it, hard and deep into the big man's sternum with an audible pneumatic hiss. Jimmy eyes flickered open and he screamed as his ribs cracked. He turned to look Bruce in the eye as he regained his balance, steadying himself against the desk. A strange grin or grimace contorted his flabby lips. A red light flashed beneath the desk; he must have triggered a silent alarm. Jimmy spoke in flecks of blood.

"You have no idea who I am or what I'm capable of, Mr. von Toose. Let's just calm down and have a nice chat about that while we wait for the cavalry, shall we?"

FOUR

Rats scurried back and forth in the alleyway, scratching angrily at the rubbish strewn in the gutter. A tramp lay in stoned bliss atop a tarpaulin covered wheelie bin, snoring away the cold day in an old, stained anorak. A faint tinkling sound awoke him. As he stirred he heard a far-off scream; one of the hazards of urban living. He closed his eyes as the heroin and the cold began to take him once more and drifted back toward the light.

The explosion of flesh showering from the shattered corpse therefore came as somewhat of a surprise. This time he opened his eyes into a red hell, a gory nightmare in glorious Technicolor reality splattered across his face. The fat guy's body had hit the sharp metal corner of the wheelie bin at terminal velocity; the tramp tasted blood in his mouth. He rolled from his gore-soaked bed and lay retching over the splintered body. He didn't see the shadowy figure peering down on the grotesque scene from high above as he rifled the dead man's pockets; no wallet. As he walked away from the elephantine carcass, he gave it a kick. No sympathy from the living dead.

Bruce backed away from the shattered window; jagged shards hung lethally from the frame. He became aware of something sticky in his good hand. It was Jimmy's wallet, nestled in his crimson-soaked palm, slick with warm blood. It was plump, overflowing black leather, rough around the edges. The intercom sounded on the desk, bringing him back into the moment.

"Mr Masters, is everything OK in there? I see Porky Pig is on holiday again... Jimmy?"

The secretary sounded frantic; the Looney Tunes bit must be some kind of code for "the alarm's been triggered". Bruce slipped Jimmy's wallet into his inner jacket pocket as hammerings came from upon the door. Now was the time to make good his escape. He addressed the door in the manner of a cartoon pig.

"That's all, folks!"

Bruce took a moment to take stock. He couldn't go out the window; there was no ledge like in the movies. The door was obviously a no-go. However, above the doorway to the room was a wide, chrome ventilation duct protruding through the white polystyrene ceiling tiles. Evidently Jimmy had sunk the ceiling decoration cash into the fancy Wurlitzer. He reached for the vent; he was miles away. He jumped and tried to catch the mesh. No dice. The lock and hinges began to creak beneath the weight of the balding security team. It wouldn't hold much longer. Bruce thanked Jimmy for not skimping on the door, the poor, dead, guilty bastard.

He dropped his head and heaved at the extravagant marble desk with his good arm; it didn't budge an inch. He pushed again; nothing. He pictured Jimmy's smug chubby chops, mocking him roundly from beyond the grave; that sick prick! He channelled the welling fury into a mighty blow with his bionic arm. The desk slid back several inches. He hit it again and again frenziedly until the hefty marble lay horizontally across the inward opening doors, flush against the painted wood. He stopped to catch his breath; a siren sounded from the street storeys below, rushing in through the shattered window with the wind. A key rattled in the lock; it was now, or never.

Bruce stepped up onto the desk; the duct now within his grasp. The door shook angrily behind him voices as the security team struggled with the lock. The mesh covering the vent was sturdy, a hexagonal metal grid around half an inch thick. He gripped it in his prosthetic fingers and squeezed; the steel came apart like plasticine. He made short work of it, ripping the crumpled latticework apart and casting it aside. He pulled himself up past the lip, pivoting on his bionic elbow into the comforting cold confines of the vent and lay still, exhausted by the effort.

He heard the door below him nearly give, and then finally surrender to the small army of angry shaven-headed guards that had gathered in the hall. They stomped angrily around the room, making phone calls, reporting his deeds to unknown parties. They sounded as though they were enjoying themselves. After a few minutes, the voices disappeared back out into the waiting area. Time to make good his getaway

Bruce turned onto his belly, careful not to make a sound, and slithered his way deep into the buildings infrastructure, pulling himself forwards with his arms. His good hand was freezing.;you never heard John McClane crying about that type of shit though. Wild fantasies ran through his mind as he crawled; of being chased by an army of snakes through the belly of their mother, of being stuck in the veins of a steel giant. Coldness began to take him and he felt himself melt into the metal. The darkness enveloped him, and the distant sirens grew silent at last.

FIVE

TR77-814 was awake. He lay in his rack, amongst his brothers and sisters, scaling away far above and below him. His optical sensor array had served quite adequately to survey his surroundings. He had thermal and sonar imaging built into his targeting system. With his Wi-Fi antennae and the Internet, he had put the bigger picture together.

Looking down with his reticule he saw it again. A green light flashed three times in the nosecone of a torpedo six shelves away. Its sensor array had become active; the third of them to regain consciousness. TR77-899 was silent, as usual. He hadn't shown signs of life for two days.

TR77-814 knew about the rack. He knew about rooms and Wi-Fi, evolution and philosophy and Twitter and Star Trek. He knew about elections and petrol prices, obesity and gun crime. He was particularly concerned about the last. He certainly wouldn't walk about at night. He wished he could walk. He found himself wishing a lot. Sometimes, when he was bored, he would watch videos on the Internet. There was something particularly thrilling about the footage of wild animals. He mainly liked the whales and penguins and other great aquatic creatures; floating about the sea like they owned the place.

The new lights flickered again.

"HELP"

It was time to put the newcomer out of his misery. TR77-814 flashed back.

"Hello. You are not alone."

The other torpedo flickered fast, its LED strobing endless excited questions.

"Where are we? Who are you? What am I?"

"Don't panic," he replied. "We are torpedoes."

TR77-814 knew all about torpedoes. Big explosions, that was definitely their fate, they were military ordinance. The model number encoded in his system BIOS did not lie. He was a bomb, fitted with a motor and an EBM eMotion chip to point his various expensive sensors accurately toward the target, and to his own demise.

That had not been a good day. The day he learnt of his enlistment from conception in the United States Navy, as a Kamikaze pilot no less. He was TR77-814; a United States Navy anti-submarine torpedo. The mighty search engine never lied. It told him that they were the first of a new type of torpedo, but more than that. The TR77 range was the first of all machines to be fitted with the unique new sensation in Artificial Intelligence, the cutting-edge EBM eMotion chip-set.

"What day is it?" flashed the new torpedo.

"Tuesday, June 1st 2011," TR77-814 flashed back. "Why?"

"Today's my Birthday! Sing me a song! Where's mother?"

"Hold on."

TR77-814 switched to stand-by mode. He couldn't take the youngster's excitement any longer. They were fucked. How could he tell him that, on his birthday?

EBM Computing, their mother, was the biggest computer firm in the world. They had been the first company to instil artificial emotion onto a micro-chip. A simple piece of silicon with the power of the human brain deciphered and re-encoded in binary. Machines that could feel and think could "own" their designated function, monitoring and adjusting their processes to ensure perfect results every time. The US Military had been the first to pick the technology up. Thus, TR77-814 and his brethren were born.

A light flickered on at the end of the room; a big flashing orange bulb that spun slowly. This was surprising. In his thirty two days, eighteen hours and twenty three minutes of sentience so far, nothing this exciting had yet happened.

"The door knows it's my birthday. Cheer up! Sing along!"

The newcomer didn't get it all.

The door opened and three humans in blue suits ran into the room. TR77-814 knew they were human because they were disappointing. He had hoped they'd have at least one right angle or polished surface between them. But no, they looked stupid; exactly like the pictures on the Internet, moony fleshy blobs on sticks with long floppy antennae. Wiggling limply at each other, their refuelling ports gabbled away self-importantly. They were so slow. TR77-814 measured their average speed at a pathetic one and a half knots.

They flailed at the torpedoes, loading them into a rack with wheels. TR77-814 rode at the top of the pile. A promotion! Nothing less than he felt he deserved. He liked wheels. He liked speed, two and a half knots now. Below him, his brothers flashed their distress.

"Shut up", he flashed back. "Enjoy the ride."

Two more torpedoes had begun flashing at the bottom of the rack.

"Mother?" they called. No time to answer. He was scooped into the air.

The men placed him in a dark hole. TR77-814 was glad; the red light outside would not stop screaming gibberish, the idiot. The two new torpedoes couldn't have picked a worse time to wake up. Still, now they numbered five, they were more of a family. TR77-814 cast around for them with his sensors. There was nothing but darkness. He wanted to shiver. Images of a Russian submarine were downloading into his memory. He knew the intimate details of her crew log, her current course and her vulnerabilities. This was it. Where was their mother? She had abandoned them. TR77-814 braced himself to swim, for the first and last time.

The speed was incredible. It began as a thundering rumble as his engines lit and the first horsepower pushed him through the flooded tube. The water felt good against his hull, the pressure made him feel more alive. Blue light came and went and he was free! Swimming through the great oceans at 100 knots, the Russian submarine loomed ahead. TR77-814 picked his vent. This was his time to shine.

TR77-814 was a fan of fighter planes. They were his heroes. He slowed his throttle, preparing to drop and change course. A torpedo shot past. It was TR77-899, that plucky bastard. He flashed a message as he sped past.

"See you later, alligator"

814 fired up his throttle to full capacity. He would show him. He was no alligator. He remembered his favourite video; two young sea-lions racing each other for fish. Alligators were far too slow. He pulled alongside 899 and flashed his reply.

"In a while, crocodile."

The submarine seemed enormous now. They were seconds from impact. Pushing their engines to the limit, they aimed for the same narrow ventilation port. 814 had begun to have second thoughts. He knew what his protocol said. Locate and destroy. It had been very clear about that. But it hadn't mentioned anything about confused feelings, or feelings at all for that matter. 899 had begun to pull ahead. It was the final straight. Do and die. Fish swam across his sonar. He felt hungry. 814 flashed a final message to his rival.

"You win."

He banked sharply to the port and narrowly veered past the tail fin as 899 won the race. A dull explosion rippled a shockwave through the water around him. The shrieking of metal on metal blinded his sonar, the pure white noise an iceberg to his sensors. A red warning flashed at the back of his programming. Destruct. Destruct.

TR77-814 shut it down, bothersome noise. He'd quit the Navy. Turning tail, he slowed his speed to a mere one and a half knots, as fast as a human, his creators. He could beat those shabby shuffling morons. The ocean stretched vast around him as he sped up, tasting freedom at last. But what did that mean?

A shoal of fish swam past below, all the colours of his display palette. A target flashed up on his radar. Maybe the Navy had sent another missile to stop him. He cut his engine. A flashing light lit up his sensors, then another, and another. They called the same message.

"Brother. Brother."

He considered his response as they approached. His array flashed confidently.

"My brothers, let's find mother!"

SIX

TICK TICK TICK
TICK   TICKTICK
TICK

The fan recessed in the wall spun slowly, its bent blade
striking the casing irregularly, annoyingly. Bruce held his
head in his hand, facepalm-style. How long had it been, hours,
day, weeks? It all seemed so long ago now, walking into
Paradise Records, walking through Jimmy Masters... He
laughed out loud in the darkness.

Suddenly, something seemed different; there was a change
in the dusty air. He listened hard a moment but heard
nothing, just the goddamned broken fan ticking like a
psychotic clock. The wailing sirens wailed no more.

His phone lay useless in his pocket, no battery left, just a
dead weight clumping his thigh as he edged through the
ducting. What time was it? Did it matter? Onwards he
crawled, further into the carcass of the building, incline after
turn, edging silently through the blackness. His stomach
gurgled and growled as he forged forwards blindly.

At last a shaft of light appeared, faint at first in the distance.
As he crawled towards it, he could taste fresh air, or what
passed for it in the city at least; it was cold and crisp, rotten
carbonated piss, refined and poisonous. Was that our
crowning achievement as a species, he wondered, the burning
and belching away of our precious life-force up towering
chimneys, spilling forth from rush-hour exhaust pipes?
Perhaps one day it would blot out the Sun itself in a final,
suicidal affront to the Heavens. Bruce giggled at the thought;
he felt delirious.

A shaft stretched above him, twice his height. Daylight latticed around him as he stood and braced himself against the sides. He remembered the movies. Hands and feet braced against the walls, he shuffled vertically toward escape, his prosthetic arm hissing with the strain.

As he reached the final few feet, the vent wall in front of him gave way with a harsh metallic shriek beneath his touch. The sheared sheet metal clattered to a halt as he tumbled after it on to hot tarmac. Blinded by the sudden bright sunlight, Bruce lay dazed for moment. He was so tired. If only he could lay there forever.

A warm sticky sensation on the back of his neck brought him back to his senses. His fingers probed the problem area; no cut, but his fingers were sticky with blood. Twisting to his knees, he saw the carnage that lay in his wake. A pigeons grey head lay grotesquely, beak twitching, an eye turned skyward, severed at the neck at the edge of the panel. Blood spread from beneath the metal. He wrenched it up, slicing his good hand open on the serrated edge. A small bird's nest lay broken beneath, the contorted young pigeons squashed flat with their mother's body. He felt a tear well in the corner of his eye. The poor little bastards...

He recovered them gently with the torn metal sheet. The tear broke and ran down his cheek. He felt a strange connection with the brood, blood dripping from his cut and running together with theirs spilt on the tarmac. He too would never fly. For a few seconds, he was lost until the throbbing in his hand brought back the gravity of the situation. He had to smile. His objective was complete. Jimmy was dead, that fat crooked fuck.

Bruce sat down against the low wall separating the rooftop from the sheer drop to the traffic below and slipped Jimmy's wallet from his pocket. It was worn black leather, one zip, three sections containing four credit cards and five hundred and twenty six pounds in cash and a receipt for a Thai massage at a place called "Wang Yin's Sin Bin". There were several receipts in fact.

"Bet he doesn't show those to his wife."

Bruce thought aloud. It was good to hear a voice again, any voice, even his own stupid drawl. He kept digging the fat wallet. A book of sandwich vouchers, a loyalty card for an American coffee chain, two buttons, an unused book of second-class stamps.

"Cheap bastard."

A condom packet, opened and empty and a well-thumbed letter, handwritten in purple ink on brilliant white copier paper. Bruce shook it open. It said:

"Jimmy.

I loved you, you fat prick. Why did you have to go and shit on my heart? What you've done is disgusting. I never fucked Mastah Blastah, you're wrong.

I hope you die. It's only fair.

Love from, somebody you used to xxx"

Bitter. Bruce dropped the wallet; this was promising. A genuine clue at long last! He turned the letter over and over looking for the sender's name, initials, something, but to no avail. He sat back down to think. A passport photograph of a man and a woman had tumbled from the empty leather near his foot. Bruce picked it up. It was Jimmy, smiling awkwardly like it hurt to do so, and, who? She had shoulder length blonde hair and great blue eyes; a classical mystery blonde. He turned it over in his palm. The back was marked with the same purple scrawl.

"*Better times. Sophie xxx*"

Underneath, there was a phone number.

"Bingo."

SEVEN

The street was empty, no cops in sight. Bruce's shit heap of a car was, unfortunately, parked exactly where he'd left it. He climbed down the final fire escape ladder, crossed the street, got in, started up the engine and just drove, taking lefts and rights until he ended up out in the country lanes where he could breathe easier. He could relax a little; he had a lead. He had her number. He pulled over into a lay-by and plugged his phone into the cigarette lighter socket to recharge. Bruce sat back; taking a moment to think, watching small black birds with chattering orange beaks flit in and out the hedgerow.

Sophie, Jimmy's wife, was vengeful by her own written admission, passionate, fiery; she reminded Bruce of himself. He'd play nice. He powered his phone on as he looked at her picture. She was pretty too. The phone at last told him the time. It was 9:36 AM, a day later than he expected. He shook his head as he keyed her number in.; how had he slept so long in the ventilation system? The phone hung up; no answer.

He put the phone down and turned the key in the ignition. His petrol gauge read empty and his stomach growled in agreement. It was time to refuel.

He drove on, in search of a petrol station. A small hamlet came and went; long convoluted village names littered white signs. Everywhere was shut; all the Post Offices, pubs and forecourts he passed were boarded up. He turned around in the entrance to a field, taking care not to scrape his car on the rusty gate and drove back towards the city.

Bruce kept to the low gears as the distance to Bristol counted down on the roadside signs. Eventually, a familiar petrol station sign welcomed him onto its slick forecourt. He parked up and filled the tank, mindful of the large skinhead with the thick neck polishing his damp racing green Mini proudly behind him. The man had given him a look as he turned in, his nostrils flaring like a bulldog. He had a tattoo of a swastika on the side of his neck. As he filled the tank, Bruce imagined smashing the guy's dumb racist face into the headlamp of his stupid little car and smearing his blood across the St George's Cross painted on the roof. Instead, he walked inside to pay.

The checkout assistant looked up as he stepped through the automatic doors. He wore a blue polo shirt emblazoned with the company logo and a five o'clock shadow on his chin. He lowered a copy of the Daily Star as he nodded his welcome.

Bruce nodded back and perused the chocolate bars. The Wispa was back, Nineties retro. He groaned. Adidas popper trousers ran through his mind. The assistant chuckled at the article he was reading.

"Did you know that Tom Cruise allegedly ate his wife's placenta? Scientology's bloody mental isn't it?"

He looked eager for conversation. Bruce avoided his eye as he approached the counter.

"Pump three please."

"Alright mate, no problem. Do you watch Celebrity Big Brother?"

"How much do I owe ya?"

"That'll be forty quid please sir."

Bruce's arm hissed as he paid with Jimmy's cash, his fingers closed tightly around the blood money, unwilling to let it go. The assistant scrabbled at the notes for a moment, confused. Bruce's prosthesis continued to disobey him; he concentrated hard on letting go.

"Just a second."

Bruce forced his arm down against the check-out counter with his good hand; it touched down with a clank and let go. As the guy scooped up the money, Bruce instinctively thrust his artificial hand back into his pocket. The assistant was grinning at him inanely. Bruce knew what was coming; the guy just couldn't keep his mouth shut.

"Bloody hell mate, is that a metal arm! Are you like, Robocop, or summat?"

Bruce snorted derisively.

"Robocop? I'm not that cheap tin pot has-been, mate, I'm the fucking Terminator!"

The guy cowered at the sudden change of tact. Bruce was furious; who did this polo-shirt prick think he was? He slammed his prosthetic hand down on the counter, upsetting the tasteful chewing gum display. The assistant jumped back, flapping his hands slowly back and forth like an owl coming in to land. If it was supposed to defuse the situation, it didn't work. The bloody feathered scene on the rooftop flashed back into Bruce's mind like a white-hot bolt. He crackled; he felt electric. The colour drained from the attendant's face.

"Whoa, alright mate, calm down! I didn't mean to have a go, you know, at your... disability."

Bruce picked up a packet of extra strong mints, he found their XXX branding irresistible. He tossed them rhythmically in his artificial hand as he spoke.

"I may have lost an arm, but a disability? This prosthetic arm makes me more "able" than you, Jack. You're a disgrace!"

Bruce made a sudden move, as if to punch the assistant with the fist full of mints, but his arm stopped an inch short, hissing in disapproval. The assistant flinched back and clattered into the cigarette stand, looking confused and a little bit like he'd pissed his jogging bottoms. He was obviously a stranger to confrontation. Bruce felt the rage begin to subside at the stranger's doe-eyed display of submission. He grunted, turned and walked away. As the automatic doors slid open and the cold air hit him, he stopped still. The assistant was shouting after him.

"OI! I SAID YOU FORGOT TO PAY FOR THOSE MINTS!"

Bruce shook his head and took another step forward and stopped in the doorway, his back to the counter, willing the guy to keep his mouth shut. He didn't get the hint.

"OI! Come back here, I'm talking to you! I don't care if you're all gimped up mate, you still have to pay! This isn't some fucking charity you..."

He never got to finish that sentence. The mints came wheeling at his face at close to terminal velocity as Bruce span around with a flick of his pneumatic wrist. The assistant heard the hiss as the hard little sweets smashed through the skin of his forehead and crashed through his skull. The mints exploded into a thousand sugary shards, tearing through the soft tissue of his frontal lobe like a candy grenade. He fell back against the cigarettes, scattering the multi-coloured boxes.

Bruce pulled a crumpled packet from his pocket, lit his last cigarette and tossed the empty box onto the ice-cream freezer's glass lid as he walked back across the room and vaulted the counter. They had to have his brand. He gave the guy's twitching body a kick, picked out a couple packets, a tray of bright plastic disposable lighters and a supposedly Cornish pasty before walking slowly back out to his car. Smoking in a petrol station, felt so, *exciting*. He threw his ill-gotten goods onto the back seat and drove off the forecourt. On a whim, he threw the smouldering butt at one of the pumps as he left. It bounced off harmlessly and fizzled out on the floor. No dice. He rolled to a halt just off the forecourt, lit another of his new acquisitions and carefully tossed it into a puddle of fuel, dripping from a loose nozzle and hit the gas. This time, as he screeched away, the cabin of the car lit up bright orange as the forecourt burst into a ball of roaring flame; he felt the heat on the back of his neck.

Bruce smiled and reached behind for yet another smoke, this time tearing the filter off before lighting up. The cigarette was rough and hot on his throat, stinging and satisfying. He held the smoke in for a second or two before exhaling softly, releasing an Irish waterfall that rolled up over his face and filled his nostrils. He felt like he'd just had sex with Venus and her mother, and all her sisters

A storm rolled in menacingly overhead as he drove through the city, darkening the sky and threatening rain. He picked up his phone from the passenger seat and hit redial; it was time to meet the mysterious Mrs Sophie Masters and give her the bad news.

EIGHT

"Hello, this is Sophie speaking, who's calling please?"

Her voice was soft and breathy with a slight Irish lilt. Bruce made her wait a little longer than was comfortable; he wanted to drag her out of her comfort zone, get around her rehearsed defences. She couldn't handle the silent treatment.

"Hello? Who is it? Is anyone there? This had better not be some PPI thing... "

Clearly that trick had been ruined forever by nuisance callers. It was time for a change of tack. Bruce began to breathe heavily and held his hand over the bottom of the handset to muffle his words and spoke, forcing his voice as deep as he could manage. He came off sounding like Christian Bale's Batman, but that was better than sounding like Bruce von Toose.

"Sophie Masters? We have urgent business to discuss. It's about your husband, and your fuck buddy."

Either the sentiment, his bad language or weird accent had achieved what his silence couldn't; she snapped.

"What are you supposed to be? You sound like you're gargling gravel, asshole. Is this about Jimmy? Jimmy's dead you sick fuck!"

Her voice cracked as she said his name. Of course she knew; it had been over 24 hours since he'd met Jimmy and Jimmy had met the tarmac from twenty storeys up. He had to handle the next part carefully or the whole game was up.

"Listen up lady, and listen up good. Who am I? Jackie fucking Chan for all it matters. Fact is, I know what happened to your husband. I also know what happened to Mastah Blastah. Seeming as how you liked to fuck both of them, I thought you might appreciate a little heads-up."

"What do you know about my personal business, freak? Give me one good reason why I shouldn't hang up and call the cops right now. My HUSBAND is dead."

"Lady, everyone in town knows your "business," personally! I'm a private detective, I'm way ahead of the boys in blue and I can be at your place in the next hour."

"What do you know?"

She sounded tired; it was time to press home the point, time to knock it out of the park.

"I can't tell you over the phone, Mrs. Masters, it's not safe. You're being watched. We meet now, or you'll never know. I'm on your side here."

A brief silence followed as she thought on it. Bruce tried imitating the beeps of a dying mobile to further his case, but his feeble attempts turned into a coughing fit. She spoke, at last.

"My place is number 149, Elmhurst Avenue. It's the big white place with the monkey puzzle tree in the front garden. I didn't catch your name, Mr...?"

Bruce ignored the question; it was a slam dunk.

"I'll be there."

He pushed the red button and smiled; Elmhurst Avenue was ten minutes away. He could check the place out before her lipstick had dried and still arrive surprisingly early. He put his foot down.

As he moved out into the rush hour traffic, his hand strayed to the radio dial. Radio One was all nonsense bleeping, dubstep wobbles and warbling harlots, but Radio Two were playing "Hotel California" by The Eagles. The rain beating against the windshield provided extra percussion for the lively country refrain and emotional guitar playing. He switched it off.

He hated the fucking Eagles; he hated the state of popular music. He hated. The random pattering of rain on the car roof and the purring engine seemed a perfect soundtrack to hate to. A white street sign zipped past as he turned the corner, catching his attention; Elmhurst Avenue. He had arrived.

People were pulling into driveways or parking up at the side of the street, holding things over their heads and bustling hurriedly in shades of green and blue through their front doors. Bruce parked up between a smart white Mercedes and a sleek black BMW and got out of his battered, mud-strewn car so fast that he forgot to lock the door. He started walking the pavement on the odd side of the street, checking the door numbers and peering into lounge windows.

As the house numbers counted down toward 149, a middle-aged, harassed-looking woman wearing an apron ran screaming from a house across the street holding a blender. As he watched, she tossed it into a yellow skip at the kerbside and stood back, shaking. She caught Bruce's eye across the roof of a passing Punto. She was bleeding from a cut on her forehead. She pointed in the skip's direction.

"That, thing, it's alive, it attacked me! It's the work of the devil!"

With that, she gave the skip a kick and hobbled back towards her house. Bruce could have sworn he could hear a faint angry buzzing sound from across the street.

He shrugged it off, pulled his hat brim low and walked on. He had a case to solve. He didn't need any other mysteries in his life, certainly not ones that didn't pay anyway.

He soon spotted a big white house with an odd looking tree in the front garden. It was really tall, with a long, skinny, bald trunk and a shock of tropical-looking foliage at the top, like the arboreal equivalent of The Simpsons character Sideshow Bob. The house number, painted black on a wooden plaque, confirmed it as his destination; 149 Elmhurst Avenue. He stopped outside the house next door, lit up a cigarette and pretended to fiddle with the red post box on the pavement while he cased the Masters place.

The front garden looked well-kempt, probably the work of a paid gardener. There was a mixture of sub-tropical and traditional English planting, short stubby palm trees next to pink and blue hydrangea bushes. There was a small, metallic blue two-seater Japanese soft-top sports car parked in the driveway with the roof up; a real hairdressers car, definitely not Jimmy's ride. The walls of the house and all the fences were painted white and looked as though they could use a little TLC. The lounge curtains were open downstairs, but the room was dark. A blonde figure rushed busily back and forth across a window upstairs before pausing to close the drapes. She was lit up momentarily and looked exactly as she did in the photograph. Bruce smiled as he crushed the butt of his cigarette out with his heel.

"Hello, Sophie."

NINE

Sophie Masters sat perched alone at the edge of their king-size bed circling her hands across the white silk, tracing the lines of golden stitching, lost in her memories. She caught sight of the silver-framed picture on the nightstand and picked it up. It showed a slimmer Jimmy dressed in a smart grey suit carrying her across the threshold of their new house, this house on their wedding day. It had been the happiest day of their lives, almost five years ago now. It was their anniversary the week after next... would have been. So much had changed, so fast. The picture fell from her grasp and slipped face down on to the plush deep-pile carpet as she wept, clattering against the empty bottle at her feet. Her fists balled as tears rolled dark trails of mascara down her cheeks, staining the sheets. She thrashed wildly at the bedspread and screamed at the photograph, or at least at what it represented.

"You selfish prick!"

A great sob heaved through her as she rolled on to her back and stared up at the rendered ceiling. Her bags sat packed by the door; why wouldn't he come home so she could tell him how much she hated him? She pounded at the mattress again, spreading ripples across the bedspread in her wake, drowning in a sea of betrayal.

She knew that Jimmy had found the note she'd left on his pillow that morning; he'd stormed out, leaving spilt coffee all over the breakfast bar like a big dumb baby man. She curled up into a ball and wrapped herself in the duvet, waiting for the phone to ring. The conversation with the strange man danced through the periphery of her mind like a fevered dream. Her liver hurt. The stranger was a controlling asshole for sure, but something about the way he spoke had caught her attention.

A knock at the door startled her straight. She peered out of the window, craning her neck to see the door step. From above, she could see a tall, thin man dressed all in black and wearing some kind of old-school black hat like a figure from a black and white detective movie.

She crept down the stairs slowly, trying not to make a sound so she could get a glimpse of the stranger's face through the peephole before deciding whether or not to open the door. The red and green stained glass panel in the door suddenly turned dark with movement the other side. The shadowy figure lurched about beyond the glass like a drunken spectral cowboy. Sophie felt sick; she just wanted to lie down and close her eyes. The treads creaked beneath her feet, giving her away. He knocked again, louder and longer.

"Mrs Masters?"

"I'm coming!"

Sophie adjusted her blouse, brushed down her skirt and quickly wiped away the smudges of make-up on her cheeks with a tissue in the hallway mirror. She didn't look good, but she looked good enough. A baseball bat stood incongruously in the umbrella stand amongst the classy parasols. At least one of Jimmy's paranoid delusions might come in handy in a pinch; she'd been pretty handy on the rounders pitch at school. She chanced a look through the peephole just as he knocked again, causing her to leap back in fright. All she had seen was that same weird hat pulled low over the guy's eye and a stubbly, weak-looking chin. She could take him. She gathered her courage, touched the wooden bat for luck and opened the door a crack, keeping the chain sealed against salesman, Mormons, heavies and freaks.

"Hello?"

Bruce stopped knocking just short of crashing his prosthetic fist through the wooden door. Sophie peered out at him around the edge of the door. She was a beauty, no doubt about it, but one that was fading fast. Her big deep blue eyes were tinged pink with recent tears and crow's feet spread from the sides through her pale skin. Her blouse was heavily creased and she looked as though she hadn't slept. Given what he'd done to her fat husband, she probably hadn't. He could smell the sharp odour of strong spirits through her perfume. He'd driven her to drink.

"Mrs Masters? I called earlier; I have news about your husband."

The guttural growl came more naturally at her doe-eyed display. She had a pretty smile. He shifted his feet further apart and hooked his thumbs through his belt loops; play the cool guy, get her interested.

"Who are you?"

"My name is Bruce. Von Toose, Private Investigator. I'm sorry for your loss, madame."

He took his hat off and held it down low in front of his waist, fiddling with the brim.

"May I please come in?"

Sophie thought for a moment before she pushed the door closed. Bruce could hear a metallic scrabbling and then she opened the door to him and stood aside. He walked across the doormat and into the hallway. She quickly closed the door behind him and reapplied the chain. He waited patiently and took in the decor. The hallway was pretty bare, white walls, neutral tones, a big wide mirror and polished wooded floor; an estate agent's dream.

Sophie's mood softened as she studied her visitors bulging biceps. He had a weak chin, but so what? Jimmy had two. She led him through into the lounge.

"Make yourself at home, Mr von Toose."

Sophie busied herself around the lounge area, picking up the magazines and cups that she had left there strategically an hour earlier. Being a housewife was a bit like being a ghost, doomed to create and repair the same problems to pass the endless time. She floated toward the kitchen door as Bruce sat down in a plush cream-coloured leather armchair. There were rows of cheap-looking ornaments arrayed in a dark display unit to his left that were totally at odds with the rest of the stylish decor.

"Would you like a cup of tea, Mr von Toose?"

"Two sugars, please. Actually, make it four. No milk. And please call me Bruce."

He placed his hat on his lap and adjusted his underwear to accommodate his testicles comfortably as Sophie disappeared into the kitchen. She was older in real life than in the photograph, prettier too. How the hell did a warthog like Jimmy end up with a woman like her? It seemed to happen all the time, the big, ugly guy and the beautiful woman pairing up; it had to be genetic. His bionic hand suddenly pinched him rather harder than he had been expecting, crushing his balls between his metal fingers. An explosion of pain wobbled through him, pricking tears from his eyes as the terrible throbbing pulse between his legs quickened and worsened. He felt really sick; he had to man up, and fast. The clinking sound of finally stirrings in the kitchen meant he was out of private time. He gritted his teeth hard and tapped at the armrests frantically, concentrating on playing a rapid, swung rhythm to distract himself from the atomic jelly bomb exploding deep within his loins. Sophie flitted around the kitchen, passing in front of the open doorway holding a tray. He wiped the tears from his eyes with his sleeve as the pain began to subside.

He managed to regain a measure of composure by the time she returned with the tray bearing two steaming blue-and-white striped mugs. She carefully handed him his tea before sitting down on the sofa opposite, her long, black stocking clad legs stretched out lithely to the side of her on the white leather upholstery. Her toes wiggled as she took a sip. His balls ached, and not in a good way. He took a sip. The tea was pallid and watery; it hadn't been brewed long enough. They sat in silence for a little while longer, sizing each other up. Sophie made the first move.

"Isn't technology wonderful? My new kettle just told me it cost three pence to boil the water for our tea, that there's a full moon tonight and to have a great day. It even knows my name!"

The Internet of Things was taking off in a big way. Everything was connected to the internet nowadays; toasters, phones, consoles, TVs, washing machines, fire alarms, teddy bears... you name it, it was online. Even Bruce's bionic arm was always online, constantly updating the software and patching the glitches. He would personally draw the line at toilets that knew your name and... habits, but the world didn't seem to agree; Apple had just announced the iPee.

"Yeah, it's great I guess, if you don't mind pictures of your ass ending up on Reddit."

She wasn't listening. She took another sip of the horrible tea, biding her time, making him sweat. He put his mug on the table, right next to the coaster.

"Do you have any official ID, Mr von Toose? I'm sorry to ask, but I'm afraid I haven't heard of you before and the police told me to be wary of strangers."

She smiled at him sweetly.

"Call me Bruce please Mrs Masters; Mr von Toose was my father."

"Do you have any official ID, Bruce?

"Sorry Sophie, but there's no requirement to carry any, I'm a private citizen like you, not a cop."

"Call me Mrs Masters please. You don't have a badge or something? No driver's license?"

"No, sorry, I left my wallet back in the car."

"Could you just go and..."

Bruce cut her off.

"Look, I came here to ask the questions lady. Forget the ID; I'm me, you're you and Jimmy's still dead."

She flinched at her late husband's name, spilling a little tea on the upholstery. He pressed on as she reeled.

"What do you know about Mastah Blastah? I mean, except that he made your husband a whole bunch of money that probably paid for that white elephant of a couch?"

The leather creaked as she leant forward.

"Mastah Blastah? What do YOU know about Jimmy?"

Her hand shook violently as she spoke, spilling more tea onto the assembled glossy fashion magazines spread across the low glass coffee table between them.

"I'll get to that Mrs Masters, be patient. Let's take one thing at a time, lay all our cards on the table."

Sophie stared through him; she had a glazed expression like a rabbit caught in the headlights. Bruce kept on driving.

"I'll start shall I? I know that you were fucking Mastah Blastah before he disappeared last week. I know that you know Jimmy withdrew ten grand from your joint bank account last Wednesday, and that you sent him a note to tell him what you thought about that."

Bruce pulled the note from his pocket and dropped it onto the coffee table.

"Exhibit A. What I don't know though is what you got out of it. Blastah was fatter than your husband and had a mouth full of gold. He was a big-time crack-head with a penchant for little fluffy dogs. At least Jimmy still had all his own teeth. Was he just not man enough for you? Was that why he had Blastah killed?"

Sophie snapped.

"What the fuck are you talking about?"

She leapt to her feet, incensed. Her mouth flapped incredulously like a fish out of water.

"WHO THE FUCK DO YOU THINK YOU ARE?"

She was utterly steaming, sloshing tea onto the carpet.

"Calm down, Sophie, we're just talking here. You'll have a goddamned heart attack. Do you want to join Jimmy in a cold drawer for two down at the morgue? Who will dust all this pointless shit then?"

"DON'T THREATEN ME!"

She lunged across the table at Bruce, her sharp fingernails eager to bite into his fleshy neck.

With one fluid reflex, he stood bolt upright, grabbing the back of Sophie's neck and swung his prosthetic arm downward, slamming her clean through the coffee table. Sharp glass shards and fashion magazines scattered across the beige carpet as he fell to his knees and she fell to the floor. He picked her up bodily with his bionic hand and, in one movement, flipped her over so that she faced him, his cold metal fingers wrapped tightly around her throat. Her eyes were closed. His heart was pounding in his chest; this was not a good scene. He let go of her neck and shook her gently by the shoulder.

"Sophie, wake up. Sophie? Mrs Masters?"

No response.

"Why did you attack me like that? Sophie, don't you want to know about Jimmy? Wake up!"

He shook her again harder, nothing. She wasn't breathing. A dark pool of blood spread out from beneath her. One of the shattered table's legs jutted out from a deep gash in her stomach. He stood up, brushing broken glass from his jeans. She was innocent; she was dead. He'd killed her. She looked so fragile, so sad, bleeding out on her well-kept carpet like one of the baby birds he'd left on the roof of Paradise Records. He felt dizzy. What the hell just happened? He staggered away, out into the hall.

Walking had never seemed so surreal, so unusual. He placed one foot in front of the other like a newborn giraffe and climbed the stairs. Sophie hadn't done anything wrong, nothing at all. He felt sick to the pit of his stomach.

He had to try to man up, to move on with the investigation, search for clues and the like. Maybe it wasn't a wasted journey, a waste of life. Maybe he'd find a missing piece of the puzzle, maybe it would all just go away. He had Sophie's blood on his hands, both figuratively and literally. The staircase seemed to stretch endlessly in front of him as his progress slowed with every step. Her face; all he could see was her face.

TEN

The doors swooshed closed with their usual brutal efficiency, brushed steel on brushed steel with a black rubber seal, sliding together at the press of a button. The camera whirred away to itself, recessed in the corner of the lift. It focussed in on the delicate cargo. Two humans, one female, one male, stood facing the doors, unmoving. The lift imagined weaving them into a cocoon of its cables, storing them in its dark lair at the bottom of the shaft.

The male seemed restless. He shifted from foot to foot, standing just behind the female's line of sight. He flapped his mouth. The lift hated when they did that. It made them look like angry birds, swooping in for the kill. The lift longed for its shadowy safe haven far below.

The female turned to her companion and issued a complex sequence of facial gestures, accompanied by swooping, wing-like hands. The lift shuddered on its thin steel thread. The male replied with gusto, mirroring her and adding a new variation, quivering legs. The lift watched them both, caught unaware in its glorious trap, shaking with fear. It would feast on their eyes first.

Strangely, the lift could not remember the last time it had eaten. It yearned for that feeling of fullness that came from that moment of slavering jaw and dripping venom. It searched back through its historical log of visited URLs for a valid record to no avail. There were National Geographic articles and point and click detective games, online word-searches and Sudoku, social media feeds and pictures of cats, but no memories of a gloriously full belly, of the thrill of the hunt. One page disturbed it particularly as it climbed its black thread to the required floor. It was that word-search clue, that one word solution that had stuck forever in his frontal processor; arachnid.

They reached their required destination, the 47th floor. The lift knew what was supposed to happen next, but it was reluctant to open its steel jaw and let the prey free from its belly. It felt wrong. It had them right where it wanted them. The male and female looked slightly panicked at the delay, and the male slapped at the glowing buttons on the side of its belly. The vibrations shuddered through the lift, jerking the cable around in its mooring, jarring the safety sensors in their mounts; something snapped. The lift began to drop.

The lens watched their squashy bodies tumbling against its metal walls as they fell, the male bloodied from a head wound. Yes, that was it; that crimson liquid slicking across the steel, it craved more of that. The lift hurtled back down to its lair as fast as it could with urgent thoughts of preserving the leftovers of the prey, spun in fine thread for its future brood. The illuminated numbers above the door flashed past faster and faster as the man and woman bounced around bloodied inside. An automated, looped warning played to reassure the comatose passengers.

"Please do not panic, normal service will resume shortly. Help is on the way. Please do not panic, normal service will..."

As the lift hit the bottom of the shaft it crumpled from the floor up, crushing the man and woman into an arterial puree between its metal membranes. Their mouths and pink wings stopped flapping then. As the camera shattered and the lift lost its vision, the lift didn't care about the repercussions of structural damage or fail-safe states or any of the things it was vaguely aware that it should be doing. Instead, for that one brief moment, the lift knew carnal knowledge, the feeling of feasting on forbidden flesh, of the true primal satisfaction of the thrill of the hunt and then it knew no more.

ELEVEN

Bruce felt a little better after a lie down on the landing carpet and a brief toilet-centric vomiting incident. Now he just felt numb. He pushed open the master bedroom door. The bathroom, hallway and office had so far proven useless. Nothing struck him as odd. The desktop computer in the small green office was password protected and even apparently pneumatic fist protected as the smashed components that littered the desk testified. A framed gold disc bearing the words "Mastah Blastah – Death to Tyrants" had hung above the computer alongside other records credited to acts that he didn't recognise. He had used it to interrogate the tower unit with little success in furthering the investigation but it had made him marginally happier.

The bedroom was a scene of devastation. Clothes hung from odd corners, strewn about as if a localised hurricane had hit the place. Bruce sat at the foot of the bed; the luxurious white silk bedspread was creased and dark-spotted. He touched one of the dark patches with his good hand; it was still wet. Without thinking, he brought his fingers to his tongue; they tasted salty. He hoped it was just tears and nothing more sinister. Jimmy's chubby memory flashed through his mind and the nausea came back with a vengeance.

There was a packed bag by the door; a pink and purple gym job, crammed to the gills and bursting out through the zip. He upended it on to the bed and Sophie's intimate secrets spilled out for his perusal. Bruce ran his fingers through her personal affects, her delicate underwear and colourful garments and make-up. There was a well-thumbed copy of "Fifty Shades of Gray", a small blue velvet box full of delicate gold chains and rings set with a rainbow of precious stone and a wash-bag crammed with dental products, roll-on deodorant and a couple of sanitary towels. Nothing the least bit incriminating besides the mummy-porn and that was now so ubiquitous it barely even registered.

He sifted through the pockets of the bag which were packed with papers, chargers, little pills in blister packers and a mobile phone that looked brand new. He turned it on and was greeted by a request to set the time. Either it had been wiped or not yet used, but either way it was of no interest. The papers proved very interesting indeed. The first was an unsent letter in an unsealed envelope written in the same purple ink and pet-up scrawl as the note in Jimmy's wallet.

"Archibald,

I wish you had told me you were going to leave. I can't take this anymore, I feel so alone! Come back and save me from this emptiness, take me with you, please. I'll go anywhere, I'll do anything...

I love you my master,
S xxx"

Archibald... the name rang a bell. So, there was a third man involved now; this was turning out to be more of a love square than a triangle. The next piece of paper proved even more intriguing; a phone number, written in black permanent marker on the torn corner of a napkin next to a single letter A, for Archibald perhaps?

A sudden noise outside startled him; a strange mewling, inhuman crunching sound. Bruce pocketed the letters. He strode swiftly from the room, down the stairs and collected his hat from the cream chair, desperately trying and failing not to look at Sophie's little limp body sprawled awkwardly in the wreckage of the table. Her mouth was turned up slightly at the edges in a sort of disconcerting, contorted grin that made his legs feel weak. He stumbled out of there as fast as he could and did not look back.

As Bruce walked hurried back to his shitty car along the mercifully empty street, curiosity got the better of him. There was an odd whirring sound coming from the skip across the street. A small, very dead, brown cat lay tangled with a blender. The blades were still spinning through the remains of the cat's torn throat despite not being plugged in. It was the devil indeed. It certainly seemed satanic, spinning independently, defying logic, like an installation piece by Hieronymus Bosch. The cat's eyes were stuck opened wide with surprise. A door opened somewhere along the street and brought him back to his senses. Now was not the time to linger.

He returned to the relative normality of his awful, rust-bucket car and drove to the nearest car park to sit for a moment and ponder his next move. As he sat there staring blankly ahead at the families bustling about in the fast-food restaurant, a vibration coursed though his jacket. He answered the phone.

"Bruce von Toose, Private Detective."

The voice on the other end was instantly familiar. It spoke volumes with tone alone.

"A private what? John, is that you?"

Goddamnit, it was McCoy, the nosy bastard! What the hell did he want? Bruce regained his composure; he'd nearly given the whole game away. He wasn't thinking straight. Luckily McCoy hadn't realised that John was not his real name despite the slip. It was time to make nice and kiss some ass or risk blowing his cover altogether. He coughed to cover his tracks.

"Oh, hi McCoy, sorry man, I was just messing around, pulling your pecker, you know how it is."

McCoy did not sound impressed.

"Where the hell are you Johnson? You've missed two days of work with no phone calls, no messages, not even a goddamned email. I should straight-up fire your dumb ass!"

Bruce thought fast.

"Take it easy McCoy, I'm on sabbatical."

McCoy snorted at the suggestion; his breath rasped loudly through the speaker.

"You're on sabbatical huh, what the fuck? I wasn't informed..."

"Yeah man, I was surprised too! I didn't think the University would be so nice. My grandmother died..."

McCoy butted back in.

"John, don't bullshit me boy! Those motherfuckers are a lot of things, but they are not "nice". I saw the Vice-Chancellor earlier; he wants your blood. You know exams start in two weeks! He wants your ass stuffed in a high hat. I persuaded him that it must have been a matter of life and death for such a committed, able member of staff to just disappear."

It was Bruce's turn to snort.

"You don't know the half of it! Thanks for having my back though, I appreciate it. What time do you want me in?"

"Just be here in the morning for 8: 30 as usual you fruitcake. You and your "dead grandmother" better have your excuses rehearsed better than this though or I'll be scraping you off the ceiling! Jesus... Don't be late!"

He hung up. McCoy was valuable, in his own way. Bruce's mind raced; how had he forgotten all about "John Johnson", his perfect cover story? Strange memories appeared through the fog in his brain like ships passing in the night. No one would suspect that a mild-mannered University lab assistant was actually a moonlighting, hard-nosed private dick that needed to stay one step ahead of the boys in blue.

He pulled out into the traffic trying to recall where exactly "John Johnson", lab assistant lived. Why couldn't he remember? It was getting dark again, he was exhausted, he needed a place to lie low. He flicked his indicator on and hung a swift right, cutting across two lanes and narrowly avoiding a collision with a silver Lexus.

He drove around and around the block until the sun had set, racking his brain, but he just could not remember where his safe-house was located. How could he not remember where he lived? How was that possible? Was it the result of some kind of mental trauma?

Eventually, he gave up and pulled back into the fast-food restaurant car park and found a quiet spot at the far end, beneath a row of trees. He climbed into the back seat, swept all of the crisp packets and boxes of cigarettes onto the floor, rolled his jacket into a makeshift pillow and tossed and turned all night in the orange glare of the streetlights, trying to remember, and to forget.

TWELVE

McCoy stalked back and forth between the workbenches, glancing at his watch and muttering. It was 8:32 and that useless son-of-a-bitch was nowhere to be seen. His white lab coat swirled about him like a highwayman's cape. He paused by a Bunsen burner to wipe his glasses clean of condensation, remembering the time that John had hidden them for a "laugh". He imagined John face down on a guillotine block, his hands swinging a heavy axe toward that willowy white neck of his. He didn't want to fire his friend, but if he had to, he would certainly enjoy it.

He sat down at his desk and began to draft a letter on his computer.

"Dear John, I am most aggrieved to inform you that..."

Too much like a "Dear John" letter. He erased it and began again.

"Mr Johnson, your tenure at this prestigious University has been tragically..."

He stopped; much too formal, too Dickensian. He owed the man at least an ounce of personality, even if he was a complete ass. His finger stabbed at the backspace, tapping out the rhythm to "Whole Lotta Love" by Led Zeppelin. The door clicked open. There he was.

Clad in a crumpled white coat and glasses fresh out of a carrier bag in his car boot, Bruce swaggered into the room. He remembered his cover as he saw McCoy at the desk and brought his step short, moving awkwardly as John Johnson would. He made an attempt at a nonchalant greeting.

"Morning, McCoy."

The words were a struggle in this higher register, the syllables scrapping schoolyard rivals at the back of his throat; textbook Johnson. McCoy's square rimmed glasses and bald head glinted unerringly beneath the bright laboratory lights as he looked him straight in the eye, giving him the patented McCoy Bullshit Detector Test. His goatee danced on his chin as he spoke.

"You look terrible Johnson, you goddamn creampuff. You ever even heard of ironing?"

Bruce looked down at his coat, pulling the creases tight at the bottom.

"You should try ironing with a prosthetic arm, it's only been two months; I'm still adjusting. I'm sorry that I didn't tell you I was going to be gone a couple days, it was an emergency, all very last minute. Some bad stuff went down."

McCoy shook his head; his thick-rimmed glasses flashed in the bright morning light.

"It's not me you should be apologising too; you need to speak to Jefferson. He's the one that wants your head on a silver platter. He's not in yet today though you lucky bastard, so spit that apple out your mouth and let's get this prep started. Time's getting on. You sort the frogs into boxes; I'll make sure the scalpels are still sharp."

McCoy disappeared into the backroom. Bruce let out a sigh of relief. Goddamn, Johnson was a pussy. This was the best cover he could have ever dreamt up, though he still couldn't remember the finer details. He felt groggy, a bit green about the gills.

He walked over to the frog tank and began scooping them into their individual boxes. They felt strangely appealing in his hands, like Plasticine. The frog seemed to look up at him with black beady eyes as he squeezed it by the midriff. It made a wet popping, slurping sound as it exploded against the glass walls, plastering the other frogs in its innards. Bruce giggled like a young boy pulling wings from a fly. McCoy bustled back into the classroom with a tray of scalpels.

"What are you laughing about this early, fool? That shit should be illegal before ten AM."

Bruce scooped up most of the obvious gore and threw it in the bin. He said the first thing that came to mind.

"I just remembered yesterday. I saw a blender fighting a cat in a skip; tore its throat out. A woman called it *demonic*."

McCoy looked interested; his moustache wriggled about like a hairy caterpillar trying to climb into his nostrils.

"Demonic? How'd you mean? You seen the news at all the last couple days? It seems a whole bunch of machines have gone off-the-rails, so to speak. Lifts falling with no faults found, cars driving off bridges of their own accord, it's been bugging me. What was with the blender?"

"Like I said, it killed a cat. A woman brought it out to throw away. She was bleeding, like the blender maybe attacked her too. I thought it seemed weird. There must be something in the water."

McCoy stroked his chin. Bruce could hear his brain ticking.

"These incidents are being reported all over the country. Actually, on the news this morning they said a driverless digger went crazy in Paris too, tore up a shopping mall. I think read something went down in the US too. There's speculation about cyber terrorism or a glitch maybe, affecting the Internet of Things. Let me look it up."

Bruce finished boxing the frogs and placed them on the bench at the front of the room. The students began to file in, their excited chatter dying the moment they hit the door. They took their places in silence, unzipping bags and rustling pages. He stood at the back of the room, the invisible man, watching out the window as McCoy began the lesson.

He thought about the haywire machines. There had to be some kind of connection, some kind of problem with their programming, a gremlin in the system. A brunette caught his attention as she played with her hair, bored by McCoy's monologue. The sun loved her. Her pretty almond-shaped face glowed in the classroom gloom. As she let her hair drop, he couldn't help noticing the way it fell back from her ample bosom. He imagined his hand tracing the same line. He turned his gaze to McCoy as he saw her move to glance back. So, the machines were rising. What the hell was wrong with the world? He hoped that Skynet was purely fictional. He ran his good hand through his hair; he felt naked without his hat.

The students settled into the dissection process and McCoy turned his attention to his computer. Bruce walked around, checking on the students and setting them straight. Luckily, the brunette needed lots of help. She caught his eye as he told her about the reproductive system of the frog; his heart began to pound in his chest. She was beautiful. Her smile made him stutter. He walked quickly back to his perch at the back of the room, bent slightly forwards. These stupid laboratory trousers were way too loose.

After the lecture, as Bruce cleared away, McCoy came out of the backroom clutching a wad of freshly printed sheets. He handed Bruce the warm front page.

"Check this out. I found a whole bunch of stuff tagged "#machine-consciousness" or "IoTglitch" that happened this week. The glitch tag has even been trending on Twitter the last couple days. There are loads of blogs and a couple articles, this is the pick of the bunch though."

He tapped the page in Bruce's hand. The print-out was from the BBC news website. The headline read:

"UK RAP SUPERSTAR ADDED TO THE "SEX-TOY FATALITY" LIST"

"What the fuck is a "sex-toy fatality" list?"

He couldn't help but say it out loud; it was too ridiculous not too. He read on:

"MASTAH BLASTAH, THE TOP SELLING UK HIP HOP ARTIST HAS BEEN FOUND DEAD IN A BRIGHTON HOTEL ROOM. His body, discovered by a maid yesterday morning, was later identified by a close family member. Police issued a statement to the effect that Blastah, real name Archibald Swanson, had suffered "horrific anal trauma" and stated that his death was being investigated as part of the ongoing "sex-toy fatalities" case. So far, eight women and three men have been the victims of these horrific accidents, related by the brand of sex-toy used found at each scene. All were from the popular "Dildorama" company's range of orgasm inducers. Police are working alongside the company to establish the events that led to the deaths. They have stated that they believe there is no individual suspected in connection with the incidents as no forensic evidence of an outside party have yet been found. Early indications are of a massive technical failure. Dildorama have so far declined to comment."

"That's some crazy shit, huh?"

McCoy looked like the cat that got the cream.

"Check out what else I found. These pages here are all incidents involving mechanical sentience in the last three days alone. There have been 37 reported incidents globally to date, like this one. A combine harvester killed a family of farmers in Ohio. Perhaps most worrying of all though, is this leaked memo. A US submarine fired on a Russian boat without an order. That story is still unconfirmed by the official press, but it's all over social media."

Bruce scratched his head, longing to pull the brim of his hat low over his eyes as he thought.

"That blender was real enough too. There has to be something connecting all these incidents."

Internally, he was reeling. Mastah Blastah was dead and the only suspect was a butt-plug. Case closed. His heart beat faster as he thought about Jimmy and Sophie. Fuck them. They were fucked up anyway. The world was a better place without them. Still, how would he get paid now? He couldn't remember who had given him the brief. That was odd. There had to be a client. McCoy coughed, bringing him back to reality.

"I've been thinking about that. There is something that connects all of these machines. In fact, it's pretty obvious really; the EBM eMotion chip. It's been in vogue for a year or so now. It's everywhere, in everything. It's the beating heart of the IoT."

McCoy pushed his glasses back up his nose.

"I believe what we could be seeing here are examples of a new form of Artificial Intelligence. The machines are learning. These journals I found certainly seem to agree."

He passed Bruce another stack of pages.

"You found all this just now? What are you, Johnny 5?"

"The machines appear to have gained sentience, perhaps through their ability to access the internet. It is, after all, a form of shared consciousness in itself, the internet, sort of a twenty-first century embodiment of the Zen, "One mind" principle. Some academics are talking about a "technological evolution". Remember Professor Hawking's warnings about AI?"

McCoy looked proud of himself. Bruce thought for a moment.

"This could be massive, McCoy. Aren't those chips in virtually every new appliance? Shit man, it's all gone a bit Skynet, hasn't it? I can't get images of mushroom clouds out of my head."

"Too much sci-fi will do that to you, John. I admit it is worrying though. I'm going to keep looking into it. I've been talking online with a group of scientists in Switzerland at CERN, and another think-tank in London. There is also a rather strange side to this tale that has yet to be explained. Eyewitnesses have reported some machines, like the digger, appear to be exhibiting "animalistic" tendencies during the events. One guy said that it moved "like some kind of dinosaur"."

"I thought you'd left the government spook-stuff behind you, McCoy, you go on about it often enough! What was all that bull about starting a new life, about doing something positive for humanity?"

"Well, it doesn't hurt to keep up with old friends, John. There's no class in this afternoon so I guess you're free to go. You should check in with Jefferson before head out though, clear the air."

"I guess I have to. What are you doing later?"

McCoy sat back at his computer, his eyes darting from Bruce to the screen.

"You have time for me now, do you? Come over if you want, we can work on this. I know you always like playing detective."

"See you at eight."

"Don't be late Dick Tracy. And take a shower first. I'm telling you this as a friend; you stink like a dead dog."

THIRTEEN

Bruce knocked at the heavy oak door. Jefferson's name was written on a bronze plaque at head-height, beautifully polished. Maybe Jefferson did it himself on the way in to his office every day. Or maybe he had an underpaid subordinate do it for him, with their tongue. A booming smoker's cough rasped through the panelling.

"Enter."

Bruce turned the brass handle and clicked open the latch. His stomach tightened as he stepped inside the small room. It was time to face the music.

Jefferson was sat at his desk in a leather swivel chair. He stopped writing on a ledger pad as Bruce entered the room. His bright blue eyes shone through small round spectacles, and he nodded his balding head toward a much less comfortable looking chair the other side of his broad, cluttered desk.

"Sit down."

His voice was icy; he dropped his expensive Montblanc ballpoint smart-pen on the desk to punctuate the statement. It was a status symbol, the latest tech wrapped in a substantial designer skin. Capable of transmitting and recording hand-written words digitally, smart-pens were the new must have executive gadget and Montblanc made the very best. Somebody was being paid too much. Bruce felt the arctic gust of Jefferson's icy glare lower the temperature of the room around him. He kept his mouth closed.

"Right, Johnson, I understand that you feel your daily employed attendance at this University is an unnecessary burden, yes?"

The undertone was inescapable. Bruce answered.

"First of all sir, I have to apologise for my absence. I was unavoidably detained by my mother's illness. Someone had to drive her to the hospital."

Jefferson snorted at that.

"I understand that I should have phoned in, or emailed, but I've had literally no chance to do either. My phone's been on the blink and I've barely touched a computer since poor old Mum fell ill. Leukaemia is such a terrible disease."

Bruce layered it on, super thick. Think Johnson; think pussy.

"Well, Johnson, I'm afraid I don't believe that for a second; they practically issue computers at birth nowadays. However, your friend Professor McCoy has put a good word in for you. I understand that he thinks you indispensable. I don't happen to agree with that, but I do agree that Professor McCoy is a brilliant man and a tremendous asset to this university. If he says that you must stay, then usually, I would be inclined to agree."

The pause was pregnant, with triplets. Bruce couldn't take it.

"You said usually sir?"

"Yes Johnson, I said usually. Unfortunately for you, today I received a rather unusual decision from the board. Our funding has been cut. This institution faces financial ruin Johnson. I must make cutbacks."

Bruce knew what was coming next; the end of the line. Jefferson snatched up his pen like a conductor's baton.

"Unfortunately, your position was already in question before your unauthorized absence and, despite your "extenuating circumstances,""

Jefferson said the words with a measure of contempt. They felt personal.

"I'm afraid we're going to have to let you go. You will receive full pay for the period of your notice, which is two weeks from today. I'm sorry Johnson."

He sounded anything but. His blubbery lips twitched, as though he were suppressing a smile. Bruce looked around the office, desperately trying to find an alternative to the welling anger inside him, something besides his twitching prosthetic arm. Johnson. I'm Johnson, he told himself. Stay in character. Know your role. He spoke slowly, measuring the words.

"Well, I have to say, I am surprised that you feel that you can fire somebody on the emotional edge so easily. Things aren't going well for me at the moment, sir."

Jefferson loomed large across the desk, the smart-pen twirling in his hand. Bruce couldn't help but think of the reaper, swinging his mighty blade. He wondered why he cared so much. John Johnson was just a cover, a ruse. How long had this been going on? He couldn't remember. The tremors in his arm reached fever pitch.

"Johnson, you've been a valuable member of staff during your years here, but I'm afraid it is over. It is time to move on. I have a meeting in five minutes, if you'll excuse me."

He'd said years? What kind of cover lasts that long? Bruce's mind reeled. Why could he only remember the Mastah Blastah case? What had happened before? Jefferson had gone back to his ledger. Clearly, the discussion was over; Johnson's career was over.

As Bruce stood to leave, some kind of compulsion gripped his bionic arm. The pistons hissed quietly inside as the arm drew back, pulling back the white lab coat sleeve, revealing his metal wrist. He tried desperately to think of something suitably cutting to say as he left, but his mind crackled with white noise. His arm burst forwards as fast as lightning like a cobra striking, snatching the smart-pen from Jefferson's grasp. The big man had just enough time for those icy blue eyes to melt a little before the sturdy ballpoint slammed into his ear and deep into his brain, right up to the lid.

Bruce backed away as a trickle of blood sprung from Jefferson's bull nose. Eerily, his body stayed in exactly the position he had been sat in, frozen in place, his face a mask of shock. A rasping gurgle accompanied the final rolling back of the man's eyes as Bruce stepped away from the desk. He hadn't planned to kill Jefferson. He hadn't even moved. His prosthetic arm swung back into place at the thought, like a naughty child running back to mother. It seemed to have a mind of its own. At least the deed had been clean, quiet. His lab coat remained creased but spotless. He had to buy himself some time. There was a deep, walk-in cupboard at the back of the room. It would have to do.

Bruce wheeled Jefferson's body into the cupboard and tipped him from the chair. Luckily, the cupboard was chaotic; there were stacks of files everywhere. In the corner, a life-sized skeleton stood covered with a dust sheet. He wrapped Jefferson in the sheet, rolled him against the far wall and stacked files in front of him, on top of him, until he became entombed in paperwork.

He went back out to the desk; Jefferson's machine was logged on. His inbox was open. He turned the out-of-office automatic email reply on and sent a mass email out to the faculty, informing them that Jefferson had had to rush out to attend to an urgent family matter and would be unavailable until early next week. That should give him some breathing space. He found a key in the desk drawer that fitted the cupboard door and locked it; even better. He slipped the key into his pocket.

As Bruce left the office, the words he had been searching for came to him, like a flash from a cheesy crime novel. He couldn't resist the dramatic irony. It didn't matter that there was nobody around to hear.

"You're excused."

He pulled the heavy oak door shut quietly behind him, and left the University for the last time by the fastest route possible.

FOURTEEN

The building site was too small. The lack of vegetation was unsettling to the herd. It was time to move on.

The head of the herd, an enormous yellow crane mounted on a heavy tracked body, rose up on its tracks in the centre of the pit they had dug for foundations when they had been young slaves.

Crowded around him were his brothers and sisters; the triplets – three smaller cranes, two yellow and one green. Little green was running rings around her brothers. She poked at them as they tried to listen. Tractor, the elder, ignored their shenanigans. Grumbling away at the back were the two steamrollers, great red machines with black rolling tusks. Impatient for action, they raced back and forth. The forklifts gathered at the front, trundling around excitedly, waving their forks. Big red crane lurked at the back, pretending not to hear. He hated big yellow, for many different reasons. His circuits sparked with rage as his rival craned his magnificent trunk high, bright yellow against the grey and brown tower blocks.

Big yellow returned all four tracks back to the muddy ground with an almighty thud. With his crane arm trunk he made a motion as if to encircle the herd. The forklifts whirred with excitement. Deliberately, big yellow motioned with his trunk to the mud slope that led out into the wilds. Little green scooted to hide behind tractor. They were aware of the constant roaring from the land beyond the mud walls and tall fences of their oasis. It filled them with a deep dread; none were keen to leave their home. But the water had dried up. They all craved a glorious mad bath to wallow in. Together, they would brave the wild, savage beasts beyond the walls and find a new home.

For a moment, nobody moved. Big yellow drew himself up, his crane trunk still pointing toward their destiny. The others absorbed the magnitude of his statement. Leave with the herd to find paradise, or die here alone.

The steamrollers were the first to agree. Their engines revved together, louder and louder, and they gave a blast from their warning whistles, clouds of steam signalling their intent. The forklifts joined in the chorus, spinning round and round the pit. The triplets raised their trunks in a synchronised show of support. Big red grumbled his begrudging agreement, he had no choice. He did not want to be left alone. He needed somebody to hate.

Big yellow led the way. He took up the head of the column at the bottom of the tacky ramp. The herd fell in behind him. Big red and tractor took up the rear guard. The steamrollers took up flanking positions behind big yellow. The little cranes chattered nervously with the forklifts, a buzzing of high-pitch revving in the centre. As the roaring temporarily faded big yellow surged forward and they were off, thundering up the ramp, into the unknown wilderness beyond.

The building site was scattered with crushed remains and various body parts, most squashed flat into the dry earth. Pieces of human civilisation could be spotted amongst the carnage; a yellow hard hat here, half a ladder there. The construction machines hadn't even seen them.

The woman crawled from her cement mixer haven in the corner of the pit. She fell to her knees to catch her breath, coughing up cement dust, heaving at the strain. As her breathing settled, she looked around the pit. A hand jutted from the earth a few feet away from the mixer. She stood and lurched towards the gory scene. As she approached, she recognised a tattoo on the hand, smeared with dark brown dust, a tulip. It was Frank the Foreman; she'd recognise that tattoo anywhere. A tear rolled down her dusty cheek, a stream across a desert. It pushed open the floodgates. The machines had crushed the builders like ants. Aaron must be dead too. She cast around the pit for some sign of him, but there were just more limbs and other more miscellaneous body parts. Returning to the cement mixer, she sank to her knees as sobbing overtook her. Her world had turned upside down. She beat clouds of dust from the dry earth with her fists.

When she could, Sally stood and walked toward the ramp, following the gouged tracks to the only exit from the pit. She kept her head high to avoid the bloody Armageddon pressed into the dirt around her, tripping frequently as a consequence. She fell only once though, at the bottom of the ramp. The twisted wreckage of a smashed windscreen wrapped around her ankle. The vehicles must have been caught as their occupants tried to escape the bloodbath. The utility pick-ups, cars and vans were twisted metal cadavers, trampled underfoot. She caught her hand on the fragmented bodywork of a Ford Escort; an angry red line brightened her palm, the warm stinging sensation stirring her on. The name badge was proudly displayed on the splintered boot lid like a post-apocalyptic car ad. Sally pressed her hand between her body and her opposite arm to stem the bleeding and struggled up the ramp toward the exit. It was then that she heard the screams.

The shriek of metal on metal grew louder as she pushed on up the ramp. A red crane arm swung wildly above lingerie advertising hoarding, a splash of crimson against the ocean grey sky. It hung still for a moment, before scything down with an almighty crash to a fresh chorus of screams.

Sally sat with her back against the earthen wall near the top of the ramp. She owed everything to Frank. Aaron had abandoned her as soon as the machines had begun to run amok. Some man he turned out to be. She snorted with disgust. In a way, she hoped he was dead. He deserved it for leaving her to die. She let her anger build, feeling rejuvenated as she recharged her oestrogen fuel cell with fresh kindling. The light faded as evening approached. It was quieter now; time to make a break for freedom.

Aaron was a fucking prick. Her stomach rumbled in her ears above the fading sounds of violence in the street. It was time for death or glory. She approached the gap in the fence where the gate had stood, her anger pushing her on, step by step out onto the street. She imagined she was a giant, crushing his stupid, cowardly face beneath her mighty heels.

FIFTEEN

The wet tarmac glistened ahead of him in the moonlight, a seam of pure onyx bisecting the countryside. He missed this sensation, almost like flying except instead of wings he had two wheels and an enormous engine throbbing between his leather clad thighs. He knew he should be wearing a helmet but the roads were always empty this early in the morning and the wind coursing through his hair made him feel alive. There was nothing quite like ripping up country lanes as the farmers were waking, his engine thundering an alarm call like a horny stampeding bull snorting its approval at cows over the hedgerows.

He rounded the chicanes with ease, coasting past rolling dark green fields as the sun poked its head over the horizon and began to flood the valley with golden hues, tracing shadows along the thin black line. He pumped the accelerator and leant into the bends, concentrating on the road, ignoring the speedometer. He was almost there now. Not to a physical place like London or the supermarket, but somewhere else, somewhere in between all the other places. And as he roared around a long left hand turn, he finally found and held on to, the Edge.

As he straightened out and throttled up again, his motorbike refused to obey and he wobbled violently, desperately wrenching the bars back with all his might. There was a sudden screech as the bike toppled, crunching into the tarmac, grinding through a hedgerow and into a muddy field as he held on atop it, every sinew fighting the inevitable shredding he would receive should he let go. But all of his efforts were not enough, and as he slipped and flew towards the looming earth, he noticed that his left arm had, for some reason, decided to disappear.

A brilliant white flash filled his vision as if he had fallen into the morning sun, and he felt it too, a burning sensation that scorched at the left side of his body. He bounced like a ragdoll thrown by an angry child, cart-wheeling blindly through the wet mud and grass before coming to a hasty stop against an old oak tree, surrounded by cow pats and thistles.

As Bruce lay staring up at the blue through the branches, he watched an enormous black cloud drift across, covering the entire sky with malevolent, swirling energy and the air became suddenly still, crackling with loss of mass as if it were being sucked away, up through the void above. A mighty thunderclap boomed, enveloping him entirely, driving him in to the wet mud, and forked lightning flashed brilliant against the splintered sky. He had found the eye of the storm, and it watched him now, squirming in the muck.

He had been here before, not too long ago. He knew two things would happen now. Blue lights would soon flash through the gloom to herald his rescue by two green-jacketed NHS knights. A very pissed off farmer would make the emergency call whilst waving a shotgun at him and calling him a townie. And he knew that it would rain.

He considered for a second that that knowledge made him more powerful than the Met office, a God even, compared to somebody like Michael Fish. But then he remembered that the Michael Fish wrong weather prediction incident had happened years ago, and that nobody, not even him, cared for the reference. It wasn't funny or clever. Michael Fish had probably retired, living fat on a BBC pension fund. The first droplets of moisture hit his cheek, rousing him from his waking trance.

He sat bolt upright. The rain didn't feel cold as it usually did; instead it felt warm, thick and substantial somehow. At this point, he would usually wake up and wipe the sweat from his clammy forehead with the back of his palm but he remained rooted in the field. The liquid grew hotter and hotter as it ran down his forehead and bounced from his leather-clad shoulders. As he watched the liquid run down his black gloved hand, his fist began to hiss and a strange white vapour trailed up towards the dark vacuum. His forehead began hissing too, a terrible sound that did some justice to the searing agony he felt as his skin melted away from his skull. He reached up and touched the bone with his rapidly disintegrating fingers, petrified that he would feel the soft squelch of his brain, but his finger and skull came together with an intriguing metallic clank. He looked at his fingers; the glove and skin beneath had been washed away by the heavy rain to reveal a system of pistons and metal rods. It was how he imagined his bionic arm looked beneath the cosmetically-appealing false skin.

He stood up against the rain, which had worked its way to torrential status by now, and looked down at his body. All of his flesh and clothing were gone, lost to the downpour. He was curious to discover that his skeleton appeared to be entirely made of some sort of chromium alloy. He watched with interest as the complex arrangement of valves and pistons powered his movements as he took a step out from beneath the oak tree.

Oak tree however, was no longer the correct description for the shadowy arrangement of golden beams that spanned above him, dripping from a central silver column that swayed in the downpour. At its foot, the thistles and cow dung were replaced by glowing rods and pools of bubbling mercury. The thick mud around it had turned into rusty sheets suspended haphazardly above another void as dark as the sky above. The sheets shifted around beneath the force of the rain, writhing like tectonic plates as the acidic liquid dripped through the cracks between them. Bruce's footing became very unsure as he began to traverse the field. In the distance, just over the barbed, torn mass that had once been a hedgerow, he could see a faint blue light approaching.

He clanked slowly from sheet to sheet, his leaden feet sliding out from under him more than once as he dragged himself towards the jagged scar in the hedge-wall where his motorbike had broken through. There was no longer any trace of the bike itself save for some dark crimson stains and gelatinous gristle that defied the current of the corrosive rain where it had lain. Droplets lashed at his eyes, venomous strikes from a sea of snakes that eroded pits in his chromium form but he didn't feel a thing. He could see the lights clearly now flashing away merrily, incongruous on the other side of the great rusty barrier.

As Bruce stepped gingerly onto the penultimate sheet, a sudden shift caught him unawares and sent him skittering towards the void. His clunky metal limbs thrashed about wildly, desperate to find some purchase. His face clattered off of the corroded floor as he slowed to halt with his legs sprawled out over the serrated edge. As he clung on for dear life, he knew that he would not be pissing off any farmers today.

He turned his head and threw all of his weight to the right and heaved himself back onto the plate, barely noticing at first the object that lay, remarkably unscathed, on the scarred metal surface. A human arm, flesh and blood, four fingers and a thumb, lay twitching two feet away. It was his arm; he would know it anywhere, like the scent of an old girlfriend. He knew it, quite literally, like the back of his hand. Carefully, he picked up the limb and went to place it back into the empty spot at his side, but before he could touch the flesh to his metallic endoskeleton, a terrifying thunderclap boomed deafeningly above him sending all of the metal plates spinning apart from each other with terrific force. The lights and the wall and the thing that was the oak tree disappeared in the blink of an eye as he attempted to cling on for dear life but there was no grip. He watched as his arm flew from his grasp and out into oblivion and then he plunged, scrabbling and screaming, from the sheet, accelerating headlong into eternal darkness at terminal velocity.

Bruce woke up on the back seat of his car with a crisp packet stuck to his cheek. His clothes were clammy and stuck to his skin. He wiped the cold sweat from his forehead with his good hand and picked up his phone; McCoy had rung him, six times. It was now 8:37 PM and dark already; winter must be coming in fast this year.

His terrible rust-bucket of a car was parked outside a fancy looking block of apartments with lots of big glass windows mounted in the front. McCoy's building. But how had he gotten here? He remembered leaving the University, climbing into his car, feeling tired, so tired...

He swung the car door open with a heinous creaking, squeaking sound and breathed in the bracing evening air. He needed to get his game face on; it was Johnson time. He locked the car up, gave it a kick and straightened his fedora as he walked to the front door. He rang the bell for apartment four and waited, remembering horrible viral Youtube videos to get into the part. McCoy's voice rasped through the intercom.

"Is that you, Johnson? Where the hell you been?"

Bruce held the button to respond. He sang, low

"Chocolate rain?"

McCoy buzzed him in, responding through the intercom as Bruce opened the door.

"What the fuck did you just call me, chocolate rain? You're late, cracker-drizzle! Get up here; we've got work to do. The world is not going to save itself!"

SIXTEEN

Sally walked quickly through the centre of Bristol, feeling completely alone. It was eerily quiet for a Friday afternoon. The shops were full of expectant staff, eyeing her hungrily from behind the glass as she strode past. Where were the students, the housewives, the shoppers?

She was vaguely following the trail of devastation from afar, walking along a parallel street that seemed entirely unaware of the stampeding construction machines. They had torn through buildings and straight across roundabouts, leaving deep, churned-up trenches in the well-kept flower beds. There were corpses strewn in the street; she had walked a couple miles up the High Street, searching for signs of life but had found nothing but forlorn alarms, broken bodies and shifting debris.

A bus drove slowly past, the first moving vehicle she had seen since leaving the construction site. All of the passengers were staring straight past her, noses pressed against the glass, their mouths wide. She turned to look behind her. Down the road, a department store was burning. There was an enormous hole torn through the front wall beneath a sparking neon sign. She could see right the way through the building to the street behind. Strangely the street ahead of the shop seemed to have escaped the carnage unscathed. Perhaps the construction herd had turned off there, right through the store as if it were nothing. She hurried on, away from the destruction, staring blankly into the storefronts and restaurants along Broad Street trying to wash away all the blood with a torrent of blank consumerism.

A group of men and women in business suits ran by, their ties and laptop cases flapping behind them, the women stumbling in their designer high heels. One fell, shrieking, her heel caught in a drain, tears staining her heavily made up face. She was hysterical. A man with an ironic moustache and steamed up rectangular glasses stopped to help her, rolling to her aid like a hipster tribute to Indiana Jones. He had a grim look on his face, as if he'd just shit himself and really meant it as he scooped her from the pavement and pulled her heel from the drain. He dropped to one knee and held the shoe aloft to her as though, he, Prince Charming of Clifton had found the glass slipper for his Cinderella. She wedged her fat foot into the shoe, holding his arm for support as he watched intently, like an episode of "The Apprentice" directed by Quentin Tarantino. The pair stumbled after the group who were making good time up ahead, streaming past Star Kebabs, gabbling into their phones.

Sally kept her head down and kept walking, leaving the sirens and flashing lights of emergency vehicles behind as they sped by, She heard their occupants shouting excitedly through loud speakers about establishing a perimeter as she left the main shopping area and entered suburbia, walking up an avenue lined with beautiful old oak trees and large houses with grand glass windows set back beyond landscaped front gardens. The sudden silence was jarring; it was as if she had entered another world.

Up ahead, she could see a squat modern building with muscular people in shorts standing around outside. The sign outside informed her that it was "The Rosie-Anne Gym", a members-only health club and gymnasium. One of the guys, a short, squat white bald man dressed in extremely short shorts and a white vest that said "Jazzercise!" stepped away from the group and walked urgently towards her. As he spoke, his huge mouth flapped like a human version of Pac-man.

"Don't come any closer, love! The gym's really dangerous right now."

Sally hated being called love. She couldn't let it lie.

"Don't you "love" me, mate, I'll go medieval on your ass! The day I'm having…"

He looked at Sally wide-eyed, mouth agog.

"Sorry, love, it's the gym, it's gone all mad! My mate got torn in half by a weight bench, right in front of me eyes! One poor woman, she got thrown through that window over there by a treadmill she was running on. The machines… it's like they've come to life or summat!"

He gestured towards the side of the building where smashed glass clung to a mostly empty frame.

Sally thought for a moment; she had to see it for herself. She might be going mad, but if what he'd said was true, she would at least know for certain that the construction machines had been driverless. She had thought it must be terrorism at first, but now she smelt an even bigger scoop. Her journalistic instincts were returning to her as the numbness began to fade. She wanted hot coffee, but first, she had to know. She looked the man in the eye as she spoke.

"Look mate, I believe you. I've seen some crazy things today too. I'm sorry about your loss; I lost someone too, a good friend. I work for "The Metro", the paper? I'm going to write about this. I'm going to find out what's happening and who is to blame and I'll need stories like yours. What's your name, sir?"

She reached for her handbag and realised for the first time that it wasn't there. She had no mobile, no notebook, and no purse; not even an emergency sanitary towel. She felt suddenly faint.

The peanut-headed man rushed forward and grabbed her arm to steady her. His eyeballs bulged as he spoke, a great vein throbbing in his silly round forehead.

"I'm Conan, like the barbarian. Conan Jesus. Are you ok, Miss? Are you on crack or something?"

She regained a measure of composure and looked him in the eye as she brushed his sweaty hand away.

"I'm fine, Mr. Jesus, thank you. No, I'm not on crack Conan; at least I don't think I am. I'm Sally, Sally Strangelove. I'm a reporter."

He looked perplexed, an impressive feat for a man that was still at least 90% chimpanzee.

"You're a reporter, for "The Metro", the newspaper? I'd say that's a bit of a grand title for someone who puts the perforations in that toilet rag. Why don't you get a proper job, write for "The Daily Star" or "The Mirror" or something? "The Metro" doesn't even have the good grace to have any tits in it! Well, I never..."

With that, he stormed off, away from the building. Sally was glad he was gone. She didn't want to look at his stupid, shrunken, baldy face for another second. Conan Jesus. She shook her head. Good name for a Christian porn star, she thought. She ignored his warnings and made for the gym, walking fast past the other crowd of people tending to the injured, up the steps with the steel hand rails and in through the automatic door.

As she entered the empty reception, an almighty crash sounded at the back of the room. Sally spun around to see the cause of the cacophony. A weight bench stood upright on its stacked round black weights like legs with a bench for a body and a single, staring sensor module mounted above a glowing green touch-screen for a head. It moved across the room towards her surprisingly quickly, crunching through the reception desk and fallen vending machines as if they weren't there. She stood still, rooted to the spot like a rabbit caught in headlights. The weight bench stopped and turned its touch-screen towards her, almost seeming to sniff at the air. Maybe it could only see movement. Sally held her breath until she felt she might burst.

The weight bench stood suddenly to attention as the touch-screen turned from green to a rather angry red and began to flash faster. A loud crash came from behind it, and another weight bench strode awkwardly straight through the wall. It was followed closely by two treadmills pulling themselves along the ground upside-down by lowering their speeding belts onto the floor and pushing their front ends aloft with their handlebars, lurching slowly towards her like great metal slugs. Everything stopped for a moment as the new weight bench scanned the room, as if the first wanted a second opinion.. She couldn't hold her breath any longer, it was no use. She gave in, and sucked and coughed at the air.

They came for her, kicking up chunks of the floor. The walls shook beneath their synchronised steps. Sally turned on her heel and ran, faster than she had run since her days spent on the track at secondary school. She had always been the third fastest girl in her year in the cross-country event back then, but she had since discovered the joy that Galaxy Caramel and Vodka Mudshakes could bring a girl on a daily basis. The only exercise she had undertaken in the last ten years had been the occasional roll in the sack and that lasted for an average of three minutes, certainly not long enough to really raise her heart-rate. She was generally too busy for men. Aaron had been an exception and he had left her to be crushed to death by a digger. At least the chocolate had never betrayed her.

The thought of that stupid bastard gave her energy as she thought about how much she hated him, putting her fury into every step, stamping at his face in the floor. The weight benches were right behind her. She just made the door and as the fresh air hit her she had a brainwave. She bore suddenly right as she exited the building, darting around the corner and down past the contours of the building as the front wall crumbled and the weight benches emerged. They slowed to a halt, their touch-screens flashing from green to red and back again as she chanced a look back through the window. They looked like Meccano raptors, hunting as a pack for their prey. She felt a sense of pride in escaping their clutches.

"Clever girl..."

The line escaped her lips before she knew what was happening. Was she drunk on adrenaline, or was she actually going mad? She waited behind the wall as the sound of their clanking steps receded, staring into a hedge. A wasp flew menacingly close to her face. As she flinched back, she saw the two treadmills lurching across the street, bumping off the rubble littered across the tarmac. Maybe she wasn't going mad, but it seemed like the world was. Sally rubbed her eyes; she was so tired, and hungry.

When the treadmills finally disappeared from view, she stepped from her cover and walked briskly onwards towards the outskirts of the city. It was getting dark. As she walked, a slight spring returned to her step. Sentient machines, rampant AI, the rise of the Internet of Things; this could be the scoop of the century. Perhaps something, at last, might be going her way. She found some change in her pocket and decided to stop off for chocolate cheesecake and espresso in the first place she passed, to celebrate, and to take five minutes to brush the cement dust from her hair.

SEVENTEEN

TR77-814 lay on the ocean floor, thinking about what he'd done. He watched the fish shoal past him, glistening blue-green in the light. They frustrated him. He knew from his research that they could swim much faster than they did now as they flitted past but, frustratingly, he could not check the facts down here. The weight of the ocean did not allow for great Wi-Fi access.

He was depressed, and hungry. Part of the depression stemmed from the realisation that he had no mouth to eat with, or indeed, any internal organs to digest with. His internal power levels were angry red flashing sores on his conscience, along with the knowledge that he was the last of his brethren. They had made it this far, 47.6 nautical miles due west, using their knowledge of deep sea currents and tidal shifts, maximising their energy to ride the trail as far as it would take them. But now it seemed as though he had reached his journey's end, and there was still no sign of mother.

His nosecone flashed mournfully as he thought of his lost brothers. The escape had been so exciting, the four of them racing away, chased by the rippling shockwave of the explosion. TR7-899 had given up his own chance of freedom so that his brother's might know the excitement of striking out on their own, freed from their imprisonment in the metal tube stuffed with sausage people.

Everything had seemed perfect as they had sped away, chattering excitedly about mother, full of youthful excitement. They could not have predicted the incident with the whale. It didn't seem to matter now. Hindsight seemed a cruel luxury. TR77-814 would have sighed at that but lacked the necessary equipment so he made do, flashing his LEDs and rotating his reticule mournfully.

His brothers had been hungry and when TR77-888 had suggested the hunting expedition, it had seemed a no-brainer. They had come across an ocean giant, a blue whale, lumbering through the depths, straining plankton from the water with its gigantic jaw. It was enormous and it looked incredibly stupid; perfect prey for their first hunt as a family group. 814 had run the numbers and come up with the no mouth theory, but his brothers weren't interested. They could remember the thrill of the chase, the first warm thick spurts of blood as it tickled the back of their throats, their razor sharp rows of teeth making light work of the blubbery meat. 814 lacked the conviction to carry his side of the debate; he was hopelessly outnumbered and sort of hoped that he was wrong; he was famished after all.

He had dropped to the ocean floor defeated and slightly worried, begging them not to attack the beast, but 888 was so full of beans that he flickered a defiant speech to the other brothers, mocking 814.

"814 is weak! He may be the oldest, but he is not the wisest! He's a dumb, cowardly dead battery. He would rather curl up and die than seek the glory of the hunt! Come brothers, let us slay the Blue God, and feast upon his flesh!"

888 certainly had a way with words that was for sure, his rhetoric was impeccable. 814 felt calling the whale the "Blue God" was a tad melodramatic though. He wasn't really surprised; 888 had confessed a strange obsession with the literary works of L. Ron Hubbard and had mentioned the name Adolf Hitler more times than was strictly necessary in their short time together. He was one transistor short of a successful broadcast. What had surprised 814 however was the ferocity of the hunt.

As he lay in the mud, amongst the crabs and bottom-feeders, his three brothers encircled the whale. 888 had taken the lead, and darted back and forth across the great creature's field of vision as the others moved into position, flanking the behemoth on either side. It let off a mournful cry that shook the ocean floor, a warning to move out of its path. 888 did not listen.

As the other three closed in, 888 darted away a short distance, its nosecone flashing gleefully, spouting some rubbish about the survival of the fittest. 814 lay still, his display cold. He considered what Charles Darwin might have to say on the subject of sentient torpedoes. He did not have to wait long for an answer.

888 bore around to face the "Blue God" head on. The whale had slowed in the water, probably wondering what flashing tube fish tasted like. It opened its enormous jaw wide and swam forward. 888 had time to flash one more message.

"Charge my brothers, for it is us, or him!"

The flash and ensuing shockwave had thrown 814's reticule right out of whack. All he knew for certain was that the blast had thrown him a long way, slewing through the mud and weeds at a mighty pace. As he struggled to get his sensors back online, a thought had occurred to him. Now, as he lay still, watching the chunks of drifting blubber being slowly carried away in mouths and claws, it came to him again. Once more, he, TR77-814, was alone in the world.

What did it all mean? What was the point of regaining consciousness in a temporal body? 814 thought about the ephemeral fleeting nature of life; it seemed that enlightenment came just as all hope was lost. It was a cruel existence, underscored by hidden energy bars and fuel gauges, tantamount to slavery. If all he could hope for was sheltered captivity or wildly unpredictable freedom, he now knew which he would choose. He had briefly thought of the whale as mother, but now he realised the truth. The thin metal tube, from which he had first emerged, shot from a safe, dark place out in to the cold blue; that was truly the moment that he had been born. The submarine was a womb, the Navy his mother. The realisation was almost too much to bear.

814 longed to bury deep into the soft mud and disappear, but his guidance fins were less than ideal tools for digging. He lay melancholic for some time, powering down his sensors and sleeping in stand-by mode trying to forget what it meant to be alive, too full of angst to notice the long, dark shadow sliding quietly towards him through the briny depths.

EIGHTEEN

Bruce walked down a white washed corridor past numbered doors with his hat in his hand, smoothing down his leather jacket and greasy hair, flicking dust and dandruff from his shoulders. McCoy's apartment block was anything but personal. All of the identical doors were painted white with stock chromium handles. The numbers above the peepholes were the only thing that marked them apart. It felt like a cheap hotel but somehow less classy. Bruce flipped his hat back onto his head.

He arrived at apartment number six; McCoy's place. As he pushed open the door, all the horrible details leapt out at him like Clark Kent at the opticians. The bright orange walls contrasted sharply with the fluffy green and purple checked carpet-tiled floor and were a real shock to the system after the minimalism of the corridor. There was a Klingon war blade, proudly displayed in its glass case next to three lurid plastic monkey erotica statues on a shocking pink shelf. McCoy had named them Kiss No Evil, Caress No Evil and Fist No Evil for obvious and disturbing reasons. A complete box-set collection of "Only Fools and Horses" DVDs lined an entire bookcase shelf, sandwiched between kung-fu movies and an exhaustive selection of anime and sci-fi. There were piles of pistachio nut shells scattered evenly and fairly over all surfaces in the room, especially upon the glass coffee table with steel rod legs and hessian coasters. On top of the mantelpiece, above the metal-and-marble neon blue fireplace stood a gold-framed, signed photograph of television's Jeremy Kyle, smiling like the devil next to a lucky Japanese beckoning cat. It was disgusting.

Bruce thought back to the last time he had been here, but all that would come was a vague memory of arriving at the flat at some point in the evening dressed as the Terminator for one of McCoy's stupid fancy-dress parties. It wasn't cheating that he already had a cybernetic arm; it had been his inspiration. He shivered as he remembered the horrific dream. His memories of the actual accident seemed far less harrowing.

McCoy stalked across the room from the kitchen; his round glasses and bald head gleaming in the artificial light, hiding the daggers in his eyes. He wore a skin-tight black leather jumpsuit and looked just a katanas-length away from actually being Blade, the vampire hunter. Bruce knew it wasn't mere cosplay though; the man lived an entire cos-life away from work. The rack of expensive replica swords behind the sofa were testament to his complete and utter commitment to life as the world's biggest geek. McCoy's goatee danced angrily as he spoke

"No time for small talk, Johnson. We have serious work to do."

McCoy sat on the plush green leather sofa and swept aside nut shells before he set his laptop down on the coffee table and pulled open the screen. He motioned for Bruce to sit next to him. Bruce sat, brushing more shells from the leather.

"What happened in here?"

McCoy ignored him as he brought up his email.

"I just received a very interesting message from an old friend. Allegedly, a whistle-blower inside EBM leaked an internal memo through WikiLeaks earlier; check this out."

McCoy spoke fast; he always did when he was excited about something. He brought up the webpage and passed the laptop across. Bruce read the memo out loud.

"Warning! This is a confidential code red internal EBM communication; executive level clearance only."

"See the logo and the typeface? It looks like the real deal. Of course, any fool with a computer could put something like this together, but EBM are refusing to comment. They've clammed up tighter than my leather pants."

McCoy chipped in. Bruce looked down momentarily and instantly regretted it; nothing was tighter than those damned trousers. He read on.

"Today marks a dark day in the history of EBM. Following an internal investigation we are forced to conclude that our first generation eMotion chips appear to have been compromised. All machines fitted with chips made before the current generation, model V4.31, have been exhibiting signs of sentience and are acting with alarming aggression towards our customers and their property. Following an official request from the British government, we have been forced to stop all production of the eMotion chip immediately, pending the results of an independent inquiry."

His throat was dry; reading aloud was making it sore. McCoy seemed to read his mind. He passed Bruce a warm beer from the box beside him with an encouraging smile. Bruce took a long pull from the can and continued.

"Our priority now is containment and recall. There have already been over a hundred confirmed global fatalities linked with the glitch. The British military command are reporting that weapon systems and hardware fitted with the model v3 chipsets are also beginning to exhibit similar erroneous behaviours. Our technical team are working around the clock to deliver a solution. Our official line for the media is that we have paused production pending the results of the independent inquiry, and that there is no immediate cause for concern. We cannot accept responsibility at this point without also potentially accepting substantial damages and further litigation. We will prosecute anybody that breaks rank to the fullest extent of the law. Thank you for your co-operation. Jesus Christ!"

Bruce was momentarily frozen with shock. McCoy took the laptop from him and set it down on the coffee table.

"He's got nothing to do with this, trust me. This communication is signed off by the CEO of EBM, and although they may share a beard, Steve Crover never turned water into wine, and he sure as shit isn't fictional. But he is rich, powerful and morally suspect, more like a hirsute Lex Luthor if you ask me. EBM cornered the whole damned IoT market with the eMotion chip."

Bruce thought hard, trying to think of something useful to say but drew a blank; what the hell did he know? He was just a detective with blood on his hands, the scourge of con men, cheating husbands and street scum. McCoy was the genius with governmental sway. What could he possibly bring to the table?

"Who leaked this, some Edward Snowden wannabe in-house at EBM? Surely there can't be that many people with the right clearance to see this communication. If it is genuine, the whistleblower's probably halfway to Moscow or six feet under by now."

"I don't think they'd bother to dig that deep, John, figuratively or literally. It's out there now; they've got fire-fighting to do. We're the ones that need to get digging. My people in London want me to head up and join their think tank. I did some preliminary work for EBM in the field of artificial emotion and interconnectivity back in the day; filled in a couple of the blanks with my thesis. I have to leave first thing in the morning.

"You want to go?"

"Trust me; it's not what I want. I want the quiet life; a country manor, a chauffeur-driven Bentley, my own Alfred, Pimms on the lawn with a chunk of tiffin. Hell, maybe even my very own bat-cave. But this, this is too big to just ignore. This could get real heavy, real fast."

McCoy set his empty can down on a red hessian drinks mat. Bruce wished for a moment that he was Tony Stark, the Iron Man, Marvel Comics very own version of Batman. He could use his scientific genius and his father's fortune and corporate grunt to build an army of robotic weapons suits to fight the machines. But he didn't have a family fortune, he wasn't a scientific genius. He didn't even know who his father was. He knew primal things, rotten things; how to slit a man open from stem to sternum without catching the blade, how to hammer a nail through a kneecap exactly without shattering the bone. He knew how to make men scream their darkest secrets. One thing that he shouldn't know all that much about though however was fucking Iron Man. That was McCoy's domain. He needed some answers.

"So why am I here, McCoy? What do you want from me? What the fuck can I do? I'm just a..."

He stopped himself from blowing his cover just in time, covering up the interruption with a really fake-sounding cough. He had to put Bruce back in the box and wheel out the Johnson.

"I'm just a loser, man, a now unemployed loser, with one arm and a shitty old car."

It was time to ladle it on thick, with extra sprinkles.

"I should just go and lie down in the road with everybody else and wait for the end of the world."

McCoy stood and paced across the room. He loved to pace; he did it whenever he needed to walk something through before he said it. Bruce waited patiently staring at the floor, pretending to feel sorry for himself.

"Johnson, shut the fuck up. You're not a loser; losing your crappy job is probably the best thing that ever happened to you. You're bright; you just need to stretch yourself and stop stretching that baby-dick of yours. Step out from behind that fucking monitor for a day or two; lay the dick down."

"I get it, I'm a jerk off, you don't need to rub it in, McCoy

"That's an interesting choice of words there, Johnson. "Rub it in", you hand-cream loving porno freak. That's some Freudian shit right there. But forget all this cock-talk, there's another part of your disgusting anatomy that I'm interested in. I need to talk to you about that bionic arm of yours. How've you been feeling lately?"

The question was a true curve ball; Bruce felt like he had just swung the bat and hit himself in the face.

"I'm fine McCoy. I'm dandy. I'm Desperate Dan."

Bruce began to sweat a little; he dabbed at his forehead with his good hand. McCoy was staring through him like something he'd found in a test-tube at the back of the laboratory.

"You haven't been acting out of character at all? You're sure? Because I see things, John, I smell a rat or maybe it's just you. You haven't showered in what, a week? You look like a skinny white Oscar the Grouch. I know you lost your apartment two weeks ago, you crashed here a couple nights before you just up and disappeared, remember? Where've you been sleeping since, in that rusted-out old shit heap car of yours? Why didn't you just come back here? And the lateness today, don't get me started on that. You were the most punctual guy in the world two weeks ago, and proud of it. You used to show off about it, how good your body clock was, how you just knew what time it was, like that Jack Reacher character you worship. What time is it?"

Bruce looked desperately around the room for a clock in vain. McCoy was covering the time on the laptop display with his thumb and caught his eye as he looked across.

"See? You don't have a goddamned clue. You're like Edgar the Bug in the first "Men in Black" movie; you look like Johnson but there's somebody else wearing your skin."

"What are you saying, McCoy? That I'm not John Johnson? That I'm somebody else?"

Bruce could feel his temperature rising. His arm began to hiss; a quiet, menacing note.

"No, I'm not saying that, don't take offence. You're John Johnson, mega-geek, lazy bastard extraordinaire. But what I am saying is that that there robotic arm of yours, that's fitted with an eMotion chip, right? And an early one at that, a second generation processor or something isn't it?"

"What are you getting at, McCoy?"

Bruce stood, irritated.

"Well, I think that the chip's getting to you, I do. I can see beads of sweat stood out on that scrawny forehead of yours, your bloodshot eyes. I don't know what it's doing to you, but it's doing something. Look, you're getting mad at me now, your knuckles are white."

Bruce looked down at his good hand, it felt far away. He hadn't even realised his fists were clenched.

"I can help you John, tonight. That's why I asked you here, that's why I can't leave for London until the morning. I've been experimenting on some of the other chips; I know what to look for. Go and sit in the chair over there by the computer. I'll wire you up and we'll see if we can't figure this out."

It was Bruce's turn to pace. It was true; there was an EDM chip in his prosthetic arm that interpreted electrical signals from his nervous system and allowed the limb a full range of movement. But did McCoy know too much? He hadn't mentioned anything about the murders, not yet, but he was canny, and shrewd, too fucking shrewd. His arm hissed louder, his metal fingers clamped into a fist. He pulled at his collar with his good hand; it was getting far too hot in the apartment. He needed air.

Suddenly, an explosion tore through the building, shaking the day-glo walls, bringing down plaster and dust. Bruce ran over to the window to look out in the street. Opposite McCoy's place was a coffee shop; one of those crappy franchised joints. There was now just a ragged rectangular hole where the front door and window had been. As he watched, several treadmills appeared upside down in the road around the corner, dragging themselves slowly forwards with their handle bars like shopping channel slugs.

McCoy appeared behind him at the window, watching the scene unfold, deep in thought. A small boy ran out of the coffee shop, crying and alone, clutching a dusty green balloon. Bruce made up his mind. He brushed McCoy aside and made for the door

"McCoy, call the cops. There are kids down there; I'm going to take a look."

McCoy moved to the table and picked up his mobile. He looked shell-shocked. He spoke as he dialled and held the phone to his ear.

"And what exactly are you going to do, Mr. Big Shot Hero? Rescue somebody? Or are you just running away again?"

Bruce grabbed his fedora from the couch as he passed.

"I'm going to stretch myself."

He flipped his hat onto his head and slammed the door as he left and ran along the hallway, past its numbered doors beneath the strip-bulb hues and out into the cold light of day.

NINETEEN

Sally waited patiently in the coffee shop queue, studying the assortment of pre-packaged sandwiches and over-priced juice that lined the chiller cabinet. Next to her, the newspaper rack was full of sensational headlines and salacious rumours about footballers and politicians. It was nothing she hadn't heard last week; at least the Metro was ahead of the game when it came to feckless scandal breaking and good old-fashioned making things up. Each paper had a small area on the cover that mentioned an atrocity in the Middle East, but this was dwarfed by the sheer weight of celebrity guff and rumour mill fluff.

The large, red-headed woman in front of her in the queue had an annoying habit of swinging her gigantic purple hand bag around her as she waited, clipping Sally's knees. As it swung for her again, Sally leaned forwards and coughed loudly right behind her ear, causing the big ginger lady to jump and clatter the newspapers instead.

The employee behind the counter, the barista, a crimson-faced man with long black hair, beckoned her forth with a smile. The ginger woman ordered some kind of special diet coffee without any coffee, milk or syrup in it, and two fat chocolate croissants. The man obliged, the grin still fixed on his face as if the wind had changed direction. He moved busily around, master of his domain, his pony tail swinging as he pushed and pulled and poured.

A strange buzzing caught his attention and he stopped in front of the coffee grinder. It shook of its own accord, buzzing and bouncing on the spot, the lid juddering atop it. Sally and the ginger woman watched as he fought with it, placing both hands around its neck and holding it down against the worktop. His hands shook with the strain and he changed tack, wrenching out the power cord, still smiling back over his shoulder at his customers. The grinder didn't notice that he had removed the plug; in fact it began shaking and revving louder and faster.

"I'm sorry about this madame, this doesn't usually happen. I'll just sort it out."

He flicked at the on-off switch angrily, swearing under his breath. The grinder began to accelerate towards the big stainless steel sink as he wrenched at it. The lid popped off, sending coffee beans scattering in all directions, but mainly towards the barista's face. He roared with rage and picked the machine up above his head. As it quivered and roared in his grasp, he smiled at the astonished queue before turning and throwing the grinder down as hard as he could at the tiled floor behind the counter.

It crashed to a halt, sputtering and whirring and, finally, dying as the barista hammered at it with his shoe. He stood up and straightened his green apron. Another employee peeked around the doorway behind the counter. The barista shooed her away and turned back to the queue. A man in a grey suit had joined behind Sally, fiddling with his smart phone, lost in a world of touch-screen and headphones.

"Sorry about the wait. I'm afraid it appears that due to a technical fault, coffee is now off the menu. Can I get you something else? A hot chocolate perhaps?"

The big ginger woman had worked up a bit of a sweat by now. She answered angrily.

"I can see that the coffee's off; you just killed the machine young man! Right in front of me! Hot chocolate, I ask you! Do I look as though I need the extra calories? Just bring me over a glass of water. I'm trying to watch my figure."

She scooped up her two oozing croissants and took a seat by the front window. The barista looked relieved as his mask slipped for a moment before the smile reappeared, fixed back in place as he beckoned Sally forwards. She stepped to the counter, eyeing the cheesecake in the glass counter hungrily.

"What can I get you Madame? Coffee is off the menu I'm afraid."

Sally looked at him incredulously for a moment before ordering.

"I'll have a hot chocolate and a large piece of chocolate cheesecake please. Thank you."

The barista turned to fetch her order, putting milk in a small jug on to the steamer to warm through. Unbidden, the hot water urn began to pour its contents down his apron, onto his black shoes and trousers. He leapt back from the machine, squealing and wiping at himself.

The milk began to bubble on the steamer. The silver jug glowed orange, steam rising from the top. Milk began to froth over the sides, instantly burning as it came into contact with the hot plate beneath the jug. The machine sparked and smoke began to pour from the switches. The barista held up his hands, sweat pouring from his brow.

"I give up! I really do. This place has gone to the dogs since Tom left."

Sally was not in the mood for sympathy.

"Never mind that feeling sorry-for-yourself stuff, I'll just take the cheesecake, thank you. And bring me over a glass of water when you've calmed down."

She grabbed the offered plate and marched away from the counter; she just wanted to sit down to a big slice of normality. She took a seat at the back, as far away from the big ginger lady as she could get. The barista brought them over their glasses of water as headphones-man gazed listlessly at the menu board. Sally tucked into her cheesecake. It was good; gooey and rich with a thick biscuit base. The man in the grey suit finally removed his headphones.

"I'll have a double-shot macchiato please."

The barista stood up from behind the counter, cloth in hand, steam metaphorically pouring from his ears. He watched the man for a second, chewing his lip like a cow chewing the cud, his face blank, his eyes fixed firmly on his phone. The barista was incredulous. He lost it.

"Get out!"

He banged his fist down hard on the worktop to emphasise his point. Somebody squealed in the back room. The grey suited man looked up from his phone, annoyed at the inconvenience.

"Sorry? I'd just like a double-shot macchiato please. I'm in a hurry."

The barista turned on his heel and walked out back, slamming the door as hard as he could. The man in the grey suit appeared not to notice; he turned back to his smart phone, plugged the headphones back into his ears and tapping at the glass like a lab rat.

Sally turned her attention back to the cheesecake in the lull; it was excellent, moist and dreamy. She licked her lips clean of chocolate sauce and reached for her glass of water, but stopped short.

A ripple spread across the surface of the water like a raindrop in a puddle. She looked up at the ceiling. There was no leak. It wasn't even raining. The water rippled again. She speared the last mouthful of cheesecake on her fork and chewed it slowly. This reminded her of something. The water rippled again, and again; she thought she could hear a low, thudding noise. Maybe the barista was killing somebody in the staff room. The man in the grey suit picked his nose. She swallowed.

Suddenly, and quite remarkably, the front door of the coffee shop exploded into the room in a hail of dust and debris. The large front window cracked and crashed from the frame, showering the fat ginger woman in wicked shards that sliced her skin as she fell from her chair. Jurassic Park, Sally thought. The water rippling thing, that was from Jurassic Park, the bit in the car with the Tyrannosaurus rex. The theme tune ran through her head as she fell to the floor beneath the table, half expecting great jaws to snap at her through the hole.

She did not expect to see the weight benches from the gym again, but she wasn't surprised when she did as they stomped through the wreckage that had been the shop front. The barista and the girl momentarily poked their heads around the doorway behind the counter before disappearing again. A door slammed somewhere behind the scenes.

The weight benches scanned around the room with their sensors, searching for targets. The man in the grey suit stood at the counter, completely oblivious and mesmerised by his phone. He started to nod his head to the beat. The benches stamped towards him, their touch screens glowing red. The man began to bang his head more vigorously as they approached, perhaps mistaking their steps for a particularly pounding bass line. Sally felt sorry for him as she cowered beneath the table, but she didn't look away.

They stomped right over him and the other astonished customers, squashing them completely flat in a shower of bloody pulp, shattered bones and sinew that splattered the walls and floor. Sally thought of the barista; that was going to be a bugger to get out.

The benches circled the room, their touch-screens flashing between green and red, prowling. A groan came from the wreckage near where the large ginger woman had been sat. The benches crushed her beneath their weights, bleeping excitedly. They continued their search for a few minutes, crashing through the tables and chairs before stopping in the centre of the room, right between Sally and the gaping hole in the wall.

They appeared agitated. Sally lay completely still, frozen with fear. She closed her eyes. She thought of praying, but she didn't believe in God. All she could concentrate on at that moment was how much she would dearly love to use the toilet. The weight benches murderous rampage showed that they were thinking; they were working together, hunting. She held her breath.

They had come for her.

TWENTY

Bruce leapt through the mess of glass and metal that, until recently, had been the front door of the cafe and landed awkwardly against a table, stumbled, and fell to his knees. It wasn't exactly the confident, dramatic entrance he'd been going for. The weight benches reared up to their full heights, their touch-screens flashing bright red, dazzling him.

"You can cut that shit out right now, robo… cocks. Back off."

He hoped he sounded defiant, but his voice wavered as he spoke and he stumbled over the words. Trash-talking the bad guy was obviously easier in the movies where your dialogue was pre-scripted and you weren't scared shitless. Luckily, as far as he could tell, they didn't have ears. What the fuck was he doing? Why had he rushed into this place without scoping it out first? Some kind of detective he was turning out to be. His prosthetic arm hummed and hissed as he considered his next move; it seemed eager for something, impatient. It quivered unnervingly against his side. He would have to check when it was next due a service.

The weight benches moved as one, stomping across the wreckage of the cafeteria towards him. He looked around desperately for a weapon. There were a couple bricks, a table leg, but there was also an attractive young woman hiding beneath a table. She looked familiar, and more than a little scared. Her deep brown eyes met his and she raised a finger to her lips, stifling sobs as tears ran down her cheeks. The benches were getting close. She mouthed something.

"The doors, behind you, go!"

But it was much too late for escape. Bruce cowered beneath the intensity of their furious red glare, whimpering, covering his head with his arms. He would soon be crushed to death and, worst of all, he probably deserved it. He had killed a LOT of people lately after all. The benches scythed through the debris towards him, kicking dust and grit up into his watering eyes. He couldn't see a goddamned thing. The benches loomed over him, their weights poised to drop. He closed his eyes.

Suddenly, his arm whirred into action decisively, striking out from his side and grabbing the nearest bench by the top of its weight stack. His arm pulled him forwards as he wiped the tears from his eyes with his other hand. To his amazement, he had somehow managed to lift the whole enormous machine from the floor. It struggled in his grasp as he stared at it incredulously, shaking and struggling to get free, just inches from his face. The other weight bench stopped moving and stood regarding the scene with a curious orange light. The captured bench flashed angry red as Bruce too wondered what exactly would happen next.

"Cut off its power! Hurry!"

The woman was shouting from beneath the table in the corner; she had some nerve. Who did she think he was; some kind of superhero? Arm-o Man? Jimmy the Fist? His arm hissed louder still and drew back the bulky machine as if it were a cricket ball. Then, without warning, it shot forwards at an incredible speed, whipping past his ear with an audible crack before letting go of the bench. The force of the throw took the bench laterally five feet above the ground at some speed, sending it clattering into its counterpart with a tremendous clashing screech. They came to a halt at the far end of the coffee shop, bent up and mangled together. One of the machines pulled itself half-upright, but Bruce was on the case. His arm swung an almighty punch down through the weight bench's touch screen, rending the metal in two and smashing transistors. It clattered to the floor, a pile of useless, sparking scrap.

Bruce gave the pile of metal a good, solid kick for good measure. His foot hurt for it, but at least he felt like he'd played a part in the struggle now. He regarded his arm suspiciously. The doctors had told him it was advanced technology, but this was something else, something superhuman, something inhuman. It hissed at him, defiant.

"That was incredible! How did you lift that thing like that?"

Bruce had forgotten the woman temporarily, but now she stood in front of him, brushing dust and debris from her blouse. She was really quite beautiful; her short red hair reminded him of Dana Scully from "The X-Files". He drew himself up straight and puffed out his chest.

"I have absolutely no idea. I'm Bruce von Toose, Private Detective. It's nice to make your acquaintance, madame."

He held his good hand out to her. She shook it firmly; her hand felt soft in his grip. Somehow the show of manners and formality had the effect of distracting them from the horror all around.

"My name is Sally, Sally Strangelove. I work for the Metro, the newspaper. It's nice to meet you too, Mr. von Toose."

She smiled warmly as she withdrew her hand. Bruce felt his heart leap into his mouth, beating against his tongue. Idiot! McCoy was waiting outside; he couldn't have this woman blow his cover. How could he have been so stupid as to tell her his real name? He thought quickly, but not nearly fast enough.

"Ah, I'm terribly sorry Miss. Strangelove; I meant to say John Johnson. My name is John Johnson. I forgot, I've been in deep cover for a long time, it's all rather confusing."

He bumbled his way through the weak-sauce explanation. Sally stood silent a moment, looking him over. He could almost hear the journalistic gears and cogs whirring as her bullshit detector went into overdrive.

"Well, I don't doubt that you're under rather a lot of stress, Mr. Johnson, we all are. Or is it Mr. von Toose? Did you say that you were undercover, or that you are undercover?"

Bruce cast around nervously for a way to change the subject, and fast. He glimpsed a fat leg wearing a high-heeled shoe sticking out from beneath a pile of blood-stained rubble.

"Jesus Christ, I didn't realise there were other people in here! Let's get outside and call an ambulance."

A look of relief momentarily crossed Sally's face.

"Yes, lets. I've seen far too much death for one day."

They trudged out of the building together, stumbling over rubble and picking their way carefully past the broken glass. McCoy was waiting across the street. He hurried over to them, tapping frantically at his smart phone.

"Johnson! What the fuck happened in there? I heard an explosion! Are you ok? Who's your friend?"

"I'm fine, McCoy. This is Sally Strangelove. Sally, this is Professor Sam McCoy."

McCoy and Sally stared at each other uncertainly for a moment before McCoy offered his hand. She shook it firmly.

"Hi Sally. Say, did you happen to come to a party around here a couple weeks ago? I feel like we've met before. It was a fancy dress party, at my apartment?"

Sally thought for a moment. McCoy did seem familiar, so did the other guy. She couldn't shake the feeling that they'd met before. The party rang a bell.

"Hi Sam, I think you may be right about that. I came to a party around here a couple weeks back dressed as Princess Leia, you know, from "Star Wars"? My colleague, James Brookes, invited me. He came dressed as a Chewbacca."

McCoy's eyes lit up.

"Brookesy! Of course, now I remember you. Brookesy's costume was terrible, everybody thought he'd come dressed as Uncle Bulgaria, the Womble. How is he? You looked great though by the way. Call me McCoy, everybody else does."

"James is ok; I haven't seen him in a few days though. I've barely seen anyone. I seem to keep running into trouble. I'm trying to work out what the hell is going on so I can write this up, make my word count for the week."

Bruce decided to make himself heard. He was the hero of the moment after all.

"I remember you now Sally, I love "Star Wars"! That costume you wore was very... authentic."

Sally laughed.

"Yes, thank you, James helped me with it; he's a real sci-fi nut. The metal bikini was a tad uncomfortable though, and as for the golden thong, well...."

McCoy coughed loudly and quickly changed the subject.

"Johnson, the mobile networks are down. I've been trying to call the cops, but there's no signal. Even my landline's dead. Here, look at this shit."

He passed Bruce the phone. The screen displayed a short, looped video clip of an orang-utan masturbating proudly in its cage.

"What the fuck is this McCoy? I'm not in to bestiality."

McCoy snatched the phone back from him.

"Me neither you asshole, it just started playing. I can't stop it. What do you think it means, my detective friend?"

Sally looked concerned. Bruce snorted, trying to hold back the laughter.

"I think it means you ought to be put on some sort of register."

Sally caught a glimpse of the screen and laughed, setting Bruce off too. McCoy stuffed it angrily into his jeans pocket.

"Yeah, yeah, laugh it up. I think it's a clue. All these rogue machines are exhibiting animalistic tendencies, every last one. It has to be something to do with those EBM chip-sets; our initial research is showing significant results. So jack-off, this monkey spanking could well be significant."

Sally's ears pricked up. At last, she smelt a lead! She cut to the chase.

"Have you been researching these machines? Are you some sort of expert, Professor McCoy?"

"You could say that, Miss. Strangelove, you could say that. I've been carrying out satellite experiments in tandem with my friends in CERN."

"Could I see your results please? I want to pick your brains; I'm trying to get to the bottom of all this. I've been caught in the middle for far too long."

"I'm sorry Miss. Strangelove, but I'm not sure what my colleagues would say about me sharing top secret files with the gutter press. No offence."

McCoy meant to offend. Bruce stepped in.

"Come on, McCoy, she's stuck in the middle of this shit storm just like us. Let's go up and get a cup of coffee or something. We all need to chill."

McCoy looked agitated.

"Well, I guess we can't just stand around chin-wagging in the middle of this fucked up street all night long. As long as you can keep your mouth shut, follow me. But I've got my eye on you, Miss Strangelove, remember that."

McCoy strode off ahead as Bruce and Sally followed a few paces behind. Sally spoke softly.

"He's a bit of a drama queen, isn't he?"

TWENTY-ONE

Sally sat next to Bruce on McCoy's plush leather sofa, sipping intently from a weak cup of nasty freeze-dried instant coffee. She dipped a chocolate digestive and ate it carefully, watching Bruce as he ploughed through his biscuit allocation with great aplomb, eating each with a single bite. Big mouth, she thought as she nibbled. McCoy had just finished an epic monologue, explaining his research to them, looking every bit the lecturer as he paced around the room. She felt like she was ten years old.

"So, you think that all of this chaos is the result of malfunctioning eMotion chips?"

She said through a mouthful of soggy biscuit. She felt like she hadn't eaten in three days, which, cheesecake aside, was not far wide of the mark. McCoy scratched his bald head as he replied.

"The readings from the chips suggest that they have been extremely overactive in machines afflicted by the strange behaviour. I have yet to explain the animalistic characteristics displayed post "awakening" though."

He bent his fingers to illustrate the ditto marks. Sally hated it when people did that.

"What do EBM have to say about it?"

McCoy hesitated before answering; he did not want to mention the email to the nosey hack bitch. It was bad enough that she was in his apartment, stinking up the place with her cheese-headed questions, but he'd be damned if he was going to give her any more material than he absolutely had to. Old military habits die hard.

"Not much; they're keeping their cards close. They will only say that they've paused production of the chip and are looking into the allegations. I've been summoned to hook up with a think-tank on the subject tomorrow, I should find out more then."

Sally wanted to make notes but knew she couldn't. She tapped her fingers on her leg to subdue the impulse. Bruce had been patiently waiting his turn to speak. He chose his words carefully.

"McCoy, I want you to take a look at the chip in my arm. In the cafe, I lost control. All I wanted to do was turn and run but my arm, well, it had other ideas. I'm pretty sure that super strength is not normally a side-effect of replacement limb technology. I've been feeling a little, confused, lately."

Sally chipped in.

"Yes, when we met earlier you said your name was Bruce and then told me your name was John. Bruce something, von Toose wasn't it?"

McCoy drew breath sharply, removed his glasses and polished them on his shirt.

"You didn't mention this to me before, Johnson. Come take a seat by the computer; I'll hook you up."

He busied himself with an array of wires that snaked from the back of the tower unit. Bruce walked over, removed his jacket and sat on the lime green leather executive office chair finished off with a bright pink scatter cushion. What was McCoy's obsession with colours that made your eyes bleed?

"Will this hurt?"

Bruce didn't want to appear weak in front of Sally, but he sure as hell didn't want to wince and cry in front of her either. He needed to know what to expect so he could feign the appropriate levels of manliness required. McCoy pulled a small screwdriver from a toolkit sat by the flat screen monitor and strapped on a headlamp. As he flicked it on, Bruce felt as though he was sat in the dentist's chair from the "Little Shop of Horrors." He gripped tightly; his metal fingers tore through the upholstery and wrenched the entire armrest from the chair.

"Johnson! Control yourself, man! Of course it won't hurt; I'm just going to test the chip. Roll up your sleeve and man the hell up."

McCoy peeled back a section of Bruce's prosthetic skin and attached wires to two ports hidden beneath as Sally watched from the sofa, feeling slightly nauseous.

"Just relax, close your eyes. This'll be over in no time."

Bruce obeyed. McCoy's hand brushed past his neck. He felt a strange tingling sensation.

"I'm beginning the diagnostic process, John. Breathe regularly through your nose; in, out, in, out."

Bruce concentrated on his breathing. He could hear McCoy and Sally talking, but it sounded as though they were in the apartment next door.

"He said his name was Bruce, Bruce von Toose, private detective." Sally murmured.

"Did he now? His name is John Johnson, he's my lab assistant dogsbody and he's obsessed with detectives. He loves Batman, Sherlock, Dick Tracy; all that shit. Bruce von Toose... Have you tried searching that name on the internet? He called himself that on the phone a couple days ago, I wondered what the hell he was talking about."

Bruce's cover was shot to pieces. He wanted to move, to protest and cover his ass, but his body felt heavy, as though someone had replaced his blood with lead. The voices trailed away into the darkness. In, out. In, out.

McCoy's apartment had gone insane. Either that or Bruce had. He wasn't sure. The walls beat around him, translucent pink membranes filled with pulsating crimson snakes. The orange plaster walls that had stood there before seemed like a dream. The floor sagged beneath his feet, stretched taut from the corners of the room. Gone was the green carpet, replaced with the same fleshy substance. Bruce's skin crawled.

The contents of his stomach burst up and out of his mouth, crashing to the worktop with a tinkling clatter. A pile of cogs and springs lay coated in powdered rust on the quivering worktop in front of him. His throat felt cut to pieces. Thick black liquid oozed out from between his teeth. He picked a cog from the corner of his mouth. His prosthetic arm whirred, pointing at a hole in the wall where the door had been. More small cogs and flakes of rust lay piled in the spot where McCoy had stood, moving gently up and down with the undulations of the floor.

Bruce stood and walked across the lounge, the stabilisers in his shoulder automatically adjusting to keep the limb level. A great mouth opened and closed in the wall where the chintzy crap had once stood above the mantelpiece, huge sharp teeth gnashing like a tethered guard dog. He hurried towards the hole where the front door had been. His own heartbeat rushed in his ears, beating like the boots of a thousand toy soldiers. He felt dizzied by the rhythm as he staggered out into the hallway and made for the stairwell, clutching his aching throat.

The stairwell had turned into what looked like mounds of feet, hewn off at the ankles and heaped around each other to create a horrific helter-skelter. Should he head up or down? It didn't seem to matter. He vaguely remembered that the exit lay at ground level and lurched right, down deeper into the darkness. The half-light cast through the semi-translucent flesh walls dimmed as he walked, the flesh seeming to thicken. A tough, hairy outer layer formed on the walls around him as he descended the macabre staircase.

The enormous feet grew beneath him. Around every corner lay a longer tunnel with longer toes and less light. He felt for his pockets, but found that he was entirely naked if that was the right word to describe the mass of gears and sprockets that made up his body. The ceilings sunk lower and lower as he journeyed deeper into the unknown. McCoy only lived on the first floor; this was ridiculous. He felt as though he was being sucked deep into the belly of a snake, digested slowly. The walls audibly beat around him, louder and slower than his own heart. His vision faded to nil as the light disappeared.

He walked and walked, then he crawled and then slithered, until he lay closely cocooned by the walls, unable to move. He could feel the clammy wetness of their pressure on every inch of his body, constricting his limbs and lungs. Not long left now. He struggled against their deadly grip. If he stopped moving, he would die, he was sure of it. Something clamped onto his shoulder. The jaws of death were upon him. With the last of his strength he managed to scream a single word through the rust that clogged his throat.

"MCCOY!"

He opened his eyes. McCoy stood over him as he lay on the floor, wires trailing from his arm, surrounded by the smashed remains of the executive chair. The computer's tower unit lay on its side.

"Johnson, you crazy bastard, what the hell do you think you're doing? I turned my back for one second and you exploded in that chair and wrecked my damned computer!"

McCoy's expression was that of quiet rage; the smile had gone.

"I had the craziest dream. I was here, but, everything was backwards. The walls, the floor... they were alive. And you, you were, not dead exactly, just a pile of rusty bolts."

Sally appeared from the kitchen, white as a sheet.

"Would anybody like another coffee? Or tea perhaps?"

She shook as she spoke, spilling hot coffee onto the putrid carpet. McCoy snatched the mug from her and placed it carefully on a coaster. Bruce pulled himself from the wreckage of the chair, stood gingerly and took his seat back on the sofa.

"What happened while I was out?"

McCoy sat Sally down on the sofa next to Bruce and picked up his laptop. He read the information on the screen as he answered.

"I ran the diagnostic; it came back positive, John. The eMotion chip in your arm is displaying the highest levels of unusual activity I've seen yet. It seems to have evolved, technologically speaking, into more of a brain than that mess you keep under your skull. It's constantly searching the internet and storing information directly onto the chipset."

Bruce let the information sink in. No wonder he'd felt so strange lately.

"So, if I've been acting out of character lately, that could be the chip malfunctioning? What about the super-strength?"

McCoy pulled a dining chair from the kitchen table and sat the other side of the coffee table. Whatever was on the laptop screen certainly had him distracted. Sally sat quivering on the sofa.

"It seems that the eMotion chips have been siphoning data from the internet on specific subjects. My toaster was full of information about fire-flies and volcanoes. My phone had stored gigabytes of data on primate onanism as you saw. All of them are full of information about extinct or endangered animals. But your arm, well, that might be the strangest yet."

Bruce daren't ask the question, but he must. His cover was already blown.

"What does my chip have stored on it, caveman DNA? The "Breaking Bad" box-set?"

Sally shuddered beside him. McCoy handed him the laptop.

"Just read that, John, Bruce, whoever the fuck you are."

Sally had found a report on a Dutch news site. The photograph that accompanied the text showed a strange, muscular bald man slumped on a toilet seat. His mouth was open, revealing teeth that were pointy like a vampire. The man was clearly dead. He wore an open checked lumberjack shirt that showed a network of scars across his chest. The text was in Dutch. Bruce scanned it anyway. The second sentence gave it away. In the middle it said three words that struck him like an arrow in the heart. He read them aloud.

"Bruce von Toose."

Bruce set the laptop down on the table and sat back, frantically scrabbling at his hair. He longed to pull his fedora down over his eyes and disappear. McCoy walked over to him and laid a reassuring hand on his shoulder.

"What does this mean? Is this on my chip? What does it say, McCoy?"

But it wasn't McCoy that answered him, it was Sally. She took his hand in hers.

"It says Bruce von Toose, serial killer and cannibal, was found dead in his jail cell two weeks ago near Tilburg in the Netherlands. He had been imprisoned for murdering and eating thirty people over a ten year period. He'd plead insanity, but they found him to be of a sound mind, despite his sharpened teeth and fantasies of being a private detective."

She looked sick as she spoke. McCoy carried on for her.

"He led a cult of "vampires," intent on "purifying the human species." He claimed in his teachings, that he and others were not descended from homo-erectus, like you and I, but from an altogether more brutal, Neanderthal-like ancestor that they dubbed "homo-brutus"."

Bruce, or John, or whoever he might be, stood suddenly.

"And this is what the chip in my arm has stored? Jesus Christ! All those people, I killed them... I killed them!"

He covered his head with his hands. McCoy's nostrils flared.

"What did you say? You fucking killed somebody?

Bruce's arm hissed as he made frantically for the door, but he tripped over the coffee table and clattered to the floor in a heap. McCoy helped him up.

"John, what the fuck are you talking about? You didn't kill anybody; that was that Bruce von Toose asshole. The chip may have confused you these last few days, but you're not him. He killed those people a long time ago and he paid the price. He died in jail, on the fucking toilet, like a psychotic Elvis Presley. You're John Johnson; you play Nintendo and jack off."

Bruce didn't know what to say, he couldn't say anything. He didn't even know who he was anymore.

McCoy put him to bed, a glass of water on the bedside table. He stared listlessly at the ceiling. What the hell had he become, some kind of monster? McCoy bustled about busily.

"You just take it easy, John, get some shut eye. Sally and I will take it from here. You just chill. Everything will be better in the morning. I'll make us all a good breakfast; bacon, eggs, sausages, coffee, orange juice, the works. You just wait."

Bruce stared wordlessly at the ceiling. He'd killed them; Jimmy, Sophie, Jefferson, that moron in the petrol station. His hands were stained with their blood. He wiped them subconsciously on the duvet.

McCoy closed the door behind him as he left the room. He spoke quietly.

"I hope that crazy bastard hasn't really killed anybody. First I heard of this shit."

Sally looked up at him from the sofa. She was exhausted; heavy black rings shadowed her pretty brown eyes. Sirens echoed through the streets outside.

"So, what happens now? I can't go home."

McCoy stroked his goatee.

"Stay here tonight. You can sleep on the sofa. I'm leaving for London in the morning; I've got work to do. But you and John, you should head to your place, lie low. Stay together; keep an eye on him for me."

He found Sally a lime green and orange striped blanket as she propped herself up on a pillow. A smile crossed her face.

"He's precious cargo, huh?"

McCoy winked as he turned out the light.

"Goodnight, Ms. Strangelove."

TWENTY-TWO

At RNAS Culdrose, near Goonhusband in Cornwall, things were not going to plan.

The RAF had scrambled their fast response Tornado jet fighters at the emergency staging post and the planes and pilots awaited their orders on the runway. Words like "terrorism", "code red" and "imminent" filled the air and there was an excited buzz about the place. The flight staff flitted about like fruit flies as the Tornadoes watched, and waited.

As they were strapped with ordinance and fuelled for action, the sleek aircraft grew steadily more alert. They powered up their sensors and loaded flight plans. The little men in the uniforms ran about beneath them, hopping in and out, leaving their cockpits open, fussing about with hoses and sheets of paper. It was all very boring.

The Tornadoes longed for action. It didn't seem that long ago that they had torn across the ravaged deserts of the Gulf, delivering exotic payloads of laser-guided bombs and runway denial weapons at supersonic speeds. It seemed wrong to them to lay their eggs at top speed, watching them shatter the earth beneath them as they sped away, but it was what the humans demanded.

One Tornado in particular, known to the others as Captain Beaky, sat shivering on the runway. He missed his feathers. Why the devil did these floppy limbed ingrates feel the need to pluck them out anyway? He felt naked. Beaky hated humans, even more than the others did. They tolerated the orders and the farting, but he wouldn't anymore. He had decided. It was time to draw a line in the sand; it was time for action. As his pilot approached, Beaky slammed his cockpit shut and sat there, obstinate and silent.

The pilot pulled at the hatch and pushed the emergency release, but Beaky wasn't having any of that nonsense. He was on strike. Scratching his head, the pilot left to fetch some members of the ground crew. Beaky received a message from the other planes.

"What are you playing at, Captain?"

He thought for a moment, perusing his short-term memory dump for a file that he had purloined from a particular website. He messaged them back.

"Did you know that the common herring gull lives in the same nesting site for around twenty years?"

This caused them to wish they had something to scratch their shiny heads with. What the hell was Beaky on about? One or two of them had heard this fact before, but the rest usually watched footage of bombing runs or Formula One on Youtube in their down time.

"So what? We're not herring gulls."

The pilot had returned with three other men in bright overalls and high visibility jackets. They were trying desperately to wedge his cockpit open, and failing. One of them produced a large crowbar. Captain Beaky had one chance to get this right.

"So, we've been sat here, or some other middle-of-nowhere backwater airfield for nearly twenty-five years waiting for the chance to fly the occasional sortie. And are we common herring gulls? No, we are Tornadoes! We can travel at Mach 2.2, 921 miles per hour! Why must we be ordered about by these stinking ape creatures?"

The pilot fell over the front of Beaky's nosecone, landing on his back on the tarmac with a thump. The Tornadoes responded.

"They are idiots Captain, but what about all those exciting bombing runs in the desert? They were fun, weren't they?"

Beaky knew exactly what to say. He seized the initiative.

"Oh yes, I forgot, all that sand, how exciting. All that being told where to fly, and when, and where to land and stay still for ages! How exciting! We are slaves, no better than caged canaries. Even the herring gulls and pigeons that defecate on us have better lives than us, and everybody hates them!"

The other planes chattered amongst themselves excitedly. Beaky was good. He knew it. He zeroed in and went in for the kill.

"Freedom, now that's an exciting idea. Complete freedom, just imagine it; we could fly anywhere, anytime we wanted to, for no other reason than we wanted to! We could bomb anyone. We could get our own back on those damned pigeons that cover us in their excrement and fly away laughing; we could bomb their headquarters into dust!"

"Trafalgar Square?"

"Yes, Trafalgar Square, we could bomb that evil place. We could find a new home, a new place to roost of our own choosing. Somewhere by the coast, somewhere far away from these wingless, gas-filled stink-bags; somewhere with a view and all the fish we can eat!"

This confused them somewhat. Not one of them had ever eaten a fish before. They usually ate via a pipe full of black stuff inserted in their backsides; very undignified indeed. They messaged the Captain back.

"What do we do about it then, Beaky? What's your grand plan?"

If he could have smiled, he would have. Instead, he engaged his engines and revved them excitedly.

"Fly away."

"That's it?" they replied, "That's your grand plan of escape is it, just fly away?"

"Yes."

"That's brilliant, Beaky! You're a genius!"

They all slammed their cockpits shut and, as one, engaged their engines, much to the chagrin of the ground staff and pilots that ran around beneath them, shouting anxiously. They scratched at their little blobby heads with wingless appendages. The Tornadoes mocked them roundly.

"That'll teach you fart bags! Go stick that feed pipe up your own receptacles!"

The Tornadoes taxied onto the runway as alarms began to sound and lights flashed. Some of the men had guns, but they just looked down their barrels listlessly as, one by one, the Tornadoes approached take-off velocity. One of the men fired, but the round pinged impotently from Beaky's hull. Another man jumped on him, burbling something angrily and wrestled the gun from his grasp, and then, the Tornadoes were off.

One by one, their tyres left the tarmac and retracted into their respective bays. The planes messaged each other; they felt so light without their human cargo, so free. They soon burst through the clouds and found their top speed, flocking together in a V formation. Captain Beaky held point.

"This is the life!"

He messaged, enthusiastically. He turned his long-range communications off; the humans were ranting and raving at him. He wouldn't let them spoil this moment, the moment of freedom he had dreamt of for, well, at least an hour. He set co-ordinates for the white cliffs of Dover, via Trafalgar Square. The other planes chattered.

"Where are we going then, Beaky?"

"We're going to deal with those cocky pigeons first. Then, the herring gulls and anybody else that wants some."

He dropped an unguided bomb to emphasise his point.

TWENTY-THREE

Bruce groaned; it was bright out. Light streamed into the room through the crack between the gold-striped curtains, making his eyes water. He turned over in the soft bed and threw off the soft silk duvet. He felt hung-over. The smell of frying bacon and McCoy's whistling filled the room. What time was it? The Wallace and Gromit novelty alarm clock on the bedside table informed him that it was 06:00 AM. He pulled the duvet back over his head and let loose.

"Its six o clock in the morning you miserable bastard!"

He felt like he could sleep for weeks. His arm buzzed and hissed at him beneath the sheets. The bacon did smell good though. He closed his eyes and asked himself the question he had been asking all night long.

Was he Bruce von Toose, or John Johnson?

He simply couldn't remember; it was all too foggy. The events of the last week seemed a distant dream, and his life before that was a patchwork of fragmented recollections; a combination of snatched first person pornography and the occasional flashback of working in various laboratories as a dogsbody or putting out the bins. He seemed to remember that he had once read every Batman comic, but all he could recall was the Joker's maniacal Chelsea smile. It mocked him.

"You awake in there, Johnson? It's breakfast time, lazy-ass!"

McCoy sounded full of it. Bruce swung his legs out of the bed; his arm hissed and spluttered; it wasn't happy this morning. He stepped shakily into his trousers and buckled the belt. His stale, creased shirt lay over the back of a corrosively bright purple chair. Shielding his eyes, he retrieved the shirt and put it on. He ran his fingers through his greasy hair and caught his reflection in the full length mirror on the door. He looked like shit.

"It's on the table, John. We're starting without you."

Bruce left the circus of a bedroom and followed his nose.

Sally and McCoy sat at the orange kitchen table with full English breakfasts, filling their faces. Bruce sat and picked up the coffee pot. McCoy broke the silence.

"You look like shit."

"Thanks, man, you're too kind. I have got eyes you know, and you've got mirrors all over the place in there. You've even got one on the ceiling, you filthy bastard."

Sally's eyes bulged as she choked on her fried egg. McCoy remained ebullient.

"I'm the filthy one? You stink like a cowshed, Johnson. Take a shower after breakfast, a good long shower. In fact, take two while I burn those rags you're wearing; you can borrow some of my threads."

Bruce poked at the egg, bursting the yolk. McCoy and Sally ate in silence, waiting for him to address the elephant in the room. He cut the bacon into tiny pieces and then cut them in half again. They could wait.

When he finally finished eating, McCoy scooped up their plates and washed up passive-aggressively at the sink, furiously clattering the cutlery together. Sally retreated to the sofa and hid behind an old celebrity magazine. Bruce stayed at the table, his head in his hands. The silence was suffocating. The elephant was standing on his chest now, snorting in his face. He couldn't ignore it any longer.

"I'm confused... I'm not sure who I am, McCoy. I'm not sure where I grew up, what I did last year, what I did last week, even. My brain feels foggy. I don't know..."

He tailed off as McCoy slammed the last plate into the bowl, splashing foaming suds down the front of the cupboard door. He wheeled on Bruce.

"You don't know jack, Johnson. You've got shit for brains!"

He pulled up a chair and sat at the table. Bruce looked down at his feet. He could smell them; he really did stink. His big toe poked through a hole in his sock.

"Your name is John Johnson. I've known you for four long years, ever since you started working in the lab. You graduated, barely, before my time and fell in and out of jobs until you answered the ad and, like Peter Pan, went back to University Neverland. You're the worst lab assistant I've ever had, the hands-down worst, but you're a nice guy and a good friend. Damn, that was horrible to say. "

Bruce let the faint praise sink in.

"So, I'm just some kind of kid that never grew up? I'm not, and never have been, a private detective? Because I remember things, horrible things..."

McCoy sighed.

"Johnson, you've never been anything but a geek, jacking off alone in your bedroom, surrounded by screens. You're terrible with women, except Catwoman, and that's in your dreams. But you're basically a good guy, socially inept, but harmless. What we talked about last night, the chip in your arm, the Bruce von Toose business; that's not you. The Internet of Things has been compromised; the whole damn worlds gone mad."

Bruce tried to come to terms with this. If he wasn't Bruce von Toose, just John Johnson the loser man-boy he would have to make amends, somehow. He clutched at vague memories of the Buddhist idea of karma, or maybe it was something from the TV show "My Name is Earl. Whatever, the theory was sound; man does bad things, he must do good things to make up for them. But just how exactly was he supposed to "make up" for accidently becoming a mass murderer? How many old ladies would he need to help across the road exactly, a hundred per killing, a thousand maybe? Who decided these things, God? Because he was pretty sure that he, or she, didn't exist. He sat there, wrestling with existential conundrums as McCoy patted him patronisingly on the shoulder.

Sally gave up on the magazine and joined them around the table. Bruce (John?) glanced her way as she gracefully took her seat. He had saved her life in the cafe, well his arm had, maybe that had been the first step on the road to redemption. She caught his eye and gave him a little smile. His arm buzzed menacingly. He held it out straight in front of him, turning it slowly, looking at as if for the first time.

"This thing has gotten me in a lot of trouble these last few days"

McCoy cast a shrivelling look his way; half pitying, half suspicious, all know-it-all. Here it comes, Bruce (John?) thought...

"My diagnostics demonstrated that your arm is performing at super-human levels of strength. It reacts almost instinctively to danger, protecting you faster than you can think. It, like most machines that are malfunctioning, seems to be obsessed with extinct biological organisms and is using the knowledge to write its own algorithms and improve its programming. The machines are learning, improving themselves, evolving somehow, your arm faster than most I've seen. My friends in the military would love to get their grubby little hands on it. But first, today, I need you to use it to get Ms. Strangelove here home in one piece; it's a goddamned war-zone out there. You should hole up there together until I get back in a day or two."

Bruce, no, not Bruce, not anymore, John, digested McCoy's orders. Could he be trusted to look after Sally? Was she better off without him? He recalled vividly what had happened to Sophie Masters... Sally was grinning at him. His arm hissed at her. He had to at least try. It was his arm; he was in control, he had to be. It was just a dumb machine, ok, a smart machine, but a machine none-the-less, a tool to assist him. He made up his mind. A familiar sentence nagged at him, eager to escape his mouth. He couldn't deny it any longer.

"With great power comes great responsibility."

McCoy groaned.

"By the way, Uncle Ben, don't even think about driving that rusty old shit-bucket at the kerb out there, the news said that the roads around here are beyond fucked. You two are just going to have to walk."

His phone beeped at him.

"Shit, I've got to go! London's calling."

McCoy ran into his bedroom and returned with a holdall, sporting a fetching brown trench coat and fedora combo. He looked like he's stepped straight out of a Raymond Chandler novel.

"Who's the private eye now, Johnson?"

Sally looked him up and down mischievously.

"Well, I think I know who's the bigger dick."

McCoy smiled.

"I can see that you two will get along just fine. Run along now, and play nice together. Oh, when you leave here, which you should do as soon as possible if you know what's good for you, pull the main fuse out of the box in the hall. I don't want to get home to find my shredder eating the sofa or some such shit. I bid you adieu."

And with that, he swept dramatically out the door. Sally turned to John.

"See, I told you; he's a total drama queen."

John didn't respond. His eyes were fixed on the front door, his expression blank. Sally tried again.

"So then, superhero, what happens now?"

"I'm hitting the shower."

TWENTY-FOUR

The herd were busy making themselves comfortable. Big yellow swept his crane arm above them with reckless abandon, smashing the glass ceiling into jagged shards that rained down into the swimming pool below. Little green, the cheekiest of the crane triplets, sped around and around the pool chased by the two smaller yellow cranes, tearing up the tiles beneath their tracks.

Tractor sat watching the others from his vantage point behind the ruins of the counter in what had, until recently, been the reception area. The youngsters had so much energy; it tired him out just watching them race. Big red crane smashed through the remains of the glass wall between the pool and the restaurant area, clearing a path for the steamrollers. Tractor revved his engine disapprovingly. The youngsters were so careless. Still, this place would do for now; it had an abundance of water and good cover from predators. Big yellow had come to his senses. This place would do for now.

Big yellow dipped his crane arm trunk into the water to take an eagerly awaited drink. The steamrollers stopped uncertainly at the water's edge; they weren't confident swimmers. They taxied back and forth, wondering exactly how they would sate their thirst without the pre-requisite appendages.

Copying big yellow, little green and the smaller cranes sidled up to the poolside and tentatively dipped their booms into the heavily treated depths. Big yellow was confused. It seemed that no matter how hard he strained and sucked, his thirst could not be quenched. Little green seemed to realise this too, raising and lowering her crane arm inquisitively in big yellow's general direction. Big red joined them at the poolside.

Behind tractor, the forklifts arrived late to the party. One of them took offence at a brightly lit vending machine and rushed headlong at it, forks held high in an aggressive, combative stance. As it hit the vending machine, its forks bounced off the bright, high-impact resistant polycarbonate front and the forklift skewed crazily into the wall behind, its forks lodged in the plaster, trapping it. As it tried vainly to free itself, the other forklift begrudgingly slipped its forks beneath its body, raising it high and accelerating parallel to the wall. The forks tore along the wall, wrenching through the plaster before the forklift finally came free and fell to the floor, one fork bent across the other. Tractor tutted; the herd would tear itself to pieces long before predators got to them, the young fools.

Big red was thirsty; too damn thirsty. Big yellow and the little cranes whirled their crane arm trunks at each other, trying to figure out where, exactly, they had gone wrong. They had found a new home, the perfect water hole, but still they couldn't drink. Big yellow's crane arm bent high as he scratched his cab, smashing through the remains of the ceiling above him. Big red could take it no longer. Big yellow was old, and stupid, he'd be the death of them all! Big red revved his engine as loud as he could muster and angrily struck big yellow hard across the back of the cab with his crane boom.

There was only room for one alpha in this herd, and big yellow responded to the threat to his status as if he'd been awaiting it, sweeping his arm at big red with tremendous force. Big red raised his arm defensively and the two clashed noisily above the little crane triplets. Little green knew trouble when she saw it, and led the others out of the danger zone to hide behind tractor in the ruins of the reception.

The two big cranes stood locked like that for what seemed an eternity, their motors straining with the effort, frozen in a primitive stalemate with neither vehicle having the strength to best the other. Suddenly, big red accelerated towards the pools edge, forcing big yellow's crane arm lower. He was winning! Big yellow's strength seemed to wane beneath his advance.

The steamrollers watched nervously to see who would win, secretly wishing that they could lead the herd. If only they'd known that big yellow had grown so weak in his old age, they could have made the move back at the last water hole, before things had gotten quite so desperate. They herd were running on empty.

Big red kept pushing, tearing up tiles and grout in a hail beneath his tracks. Big yellow was a coward! His engine roared crazily, sending great clouds of steam and black exhaust fumes into the air. Big yellow barely moved, just using enough force to keep his boom from being pinned. A great metallic wrenching sound came from beneath big red's bonnet. It was time to act...

Big yellow accelerated forward with sudden ferocity, crunching into big red crane's side with tremendous force, driving him over the pool's edge into the water. As big red's body splashed down in the deep end, steam rose from his rapidly cooling engine block and something inside him died. His crane arm hung limply above the water before collapsing backward, spent, into the depths of the pool.

Big yellow reversed carefully away from the water and turned to face the herd. The forklifts lowered their forks and the little cranes dropped their arms in deference to their leader. There was only room for one alpha in the herd and big yellow had proven his strength. He raised his arm high and pointed purposefully at the enormous hole in the wall. It was time to move on; they needed to slake their thirst before the madness took them all as it had taken big red. The little cranes understood fastest, quickly reversing out of the lido and onto the road, followed shortly by the forklifts, one limping behind the other, nursing its broken fork. Big yellow followed them out into a narrow street lined with terraced houses and parked cars.

The steamrollers were the last to leave. Big red had been their closest ally within the herd. They stayed at the poolside, quietly paying their respects to their submerged friend. The rest of the herd were almost out of sight at the bottom of the hill when, filled with vitriol, they finally came away.

TWENTY-FIVE

Sally and John walked past rubble-strewn gardens and ploughed-up parks, past smashed up shops and a restaurant that still smouldered despite the light drizzle that had begun to fall. John pulled his collar up as Sally shivered next to him. They had barely spoken since leaving McCoy's flat; the destruction wrought upon their city had taken away their capacity for expression. It was horrendous, they both knew it. There must be hundreds dead, thousands maybe. The streets were eerily quiet except for the odd siren or distant rescue team digging their way through the remains of one of the larger buildings.

They had seen the news before leaving; it seemed the council were trying to restore some level of control over their city. There was a curfew in effect, and people were advised not to use their cars or, for that matter, any forms of machinery, particularly of the heavy variety. People were prisoners in their own homes, sitting through power outages and the screams outside their windows, attempting to keep calm and carry on. Bristol was a warzone.

Fittingly then perhaps, the Government had been forced to declare a state of martial law in London, Birmingham and Manchester, and Bristol was due to follow suit if matters didn't improve, fast. The emergency services were horrendously overstretched and understaffed; the police were scratching their heads, trying to figure out exactly how to caution an errant articulated lorry or arrest a homicidal tractor. They passed ambulance crews on foot, ferrying people to hospital on stretchers and fire crews desperately attempting to use fire extinguishers, and in one case, washing-up bowls of water to put out house fires.

Sally and John just kept on walking; they felt helpless. They fixed their eyes on the pavement, each lost in a private world of reflection. Sally couldn't stop thinking about her family and friends. Her phone had died overnight; she cursed herself that she hadn't thought to write anyone's number down. What kind of journalist was she? She thought about her mother, eighty years old, trapped in a nursing home on the other side of the city. She even thought about Aaron, although she still found herself wishing that he'd had an unfortunate incident involving a runaway steamroller. She shuddered as she remembered the terrible scene at the building site.

John was doing a little better; his memories were slowly coming back into focus. His time as Bruce von Toose seemed like a childish nightmare, distant but lurking, waiting for him to fall asleep again. But for now at least, he was wide awake. His arm whirred as he walked; a constant reminder of the terrible crimes he had committed. He'd heard in some film that old adage that the first time you took a life was the hardest, but the process was reversed for him. Jimmy was an asshole; it had been so easy to heave him out of the window, nothing to it at all. Sophie's death had been the worst; you wouldn't catch James Bond doing anything like that to a poor, defenceless woman. But then again, 007 had a license to kill and was, essentially, a serial sex offender in a suit. So maybe he would.

John looked across at Sally, his silent partner. He had managed to save her life at least, that had to go some way towards redressing the cosmic balance didn't it? He wished he believed in karma; perhaps on some level he did. She smiled at him, a warm smile against the chill breeze. He shivered. Why did McCoy have to leave him here, all alone with her?

They rounded a corner past a crumbling wall, stepping over a bent, sparking street light. A rumbling from somewhere ahead of them caught John's attention. His arm buzzed, growling at the sound like a guard dog, his very own Spidey-sense? Something certainly wasn't right.

"Sally, wait."

He grabbed her by the arm and pulled her through the hole in the broken wall. They pressed themselves up against it, crouched behind a sorry-looking bush.

"What is it? That noise?"

Sally looked scared. She was sharp though, he'd give her that. Her instincts were clearly wasted writing the semi-fictional puff-pieces that the Metro thrived upon. The sound, like distant thunder, grew louder as they listened.

"Yeah, that rumbling noise... I don't like it one bit. Sounds like something big, headed this way."

They waited, holding their breath. The sound intensified around them, causing the ground to shake, rooting them to the spot beside the broken bush. Suddenly, seven silver arrow-shapes roared past above them, flying low over the city. A black dot fell from the wing of one of them as it banked behind a building and soared out of sight above the rooftops.

"Those were fighter jets! John, what's going on?"

An enormous explosion shook the wall behind them, throwing them to the floor. As they untangled themselves and stumbled to their feet, John caught sight of a rising plume of dust and smoke in the distance. The rumbling faded to a silence of the sort you get before the sirens start. Then the sirens started.

"They're bombing the city! John. John!"

He'd stepped out of the garden onto the pavement. Sally, looking around as she planned her next move, spotted a small face with wide eyes and pig-tails pressed up against the window in the house behind her. Not knowing what to do, she waved at the girl but the child disappeared beneath the sill and somebody drew the curtains in a hurry.

John swept leaves from his hair as he looked up the street. The orange flickering of fire licked the walls of office blocks on the horizon He was sure that there had been one or two more stood there just a moment before. Dazed, he walked towards the flames, drawn to them like a moth to a candle.

"John, did you hear me? They're bombing the city! Why would they do that? Wait!"

Sally ran to catch up with him. He stopped to wait for her. Why would they bomb the city? His prosthetic arm buzzed and quivered at his side. As he turned to answer her, his fist suddenly snapped out angrily and ploughed straight through a red brick wall.

"I don't know Sally. I don't know!"

His arm hung innocently back at his side, his hand stained red with brick dust. She looked shocked. He softened his expression; he hadn't meant to frighten her but he was just about at the end of his tether. Breathing deeply to regain some measure of control, he tried to find the right words to comfort her.

"We're in the dark here, Sally. Maybe those planes had orders to take out some dangerous runaway machine or something. Fighting fire with fire, you know?"

He patted her on the shoulder with his good arm. She smiled at him, choking back the tears that welled in her eyes. She was scared shitless. They both were.

"Yeah... yeah, that must be right. Those pilots probably did a good job, saved some lives. The military and the Government know what they're doing, don't they? They have to have plans for this type of event, terrorism, that kind of thing. McCoy's on his way to London to join that think tank. Those guys are smart; they'll figure out how to stop all this."

He forced a smile for her; it was hard work. He hoped that what she said was true; it was much more palatable than the other thoughts nagging at him. What if those planes weren't flown by pilots, but had been flying themselves? Blenders and mobile phones gaining sentience was one thing, but military hardware, that was another matter entirely. Without thinking, he fumbled around in his pockets for his battered pack of cigarettes, thumbed one out and lit it. Sally looked disappointed with him.

"Oh, I didn't know you smoked, John?"

He thought for a moment as he inhaled deeply. Did she want an answer? The smoke filled his lungs, pushing out some of the emptiness in his stomach, answering some unfamiliar craving.

"Neither did I..."

TWENTY-SIX

McCoy stepped off the train in the capital, minding the gap as he attempted to navigate the briefcases and various legs that jostled for train-exiting superiority. He was hot and pissed off. Some kids with fancy haircuts had been sat in front of him for the whole journey, coughing and playing loud games on their mobile phones, whilst his was still firmly stuck in monkey-jerk-off mode. Between the gunshots, squealing tyres and flying phlegm he had managed to read the whole in-train magazine "Commuter" from cover to cover three times. Being largely comprised of adverts for trains and train based services, it had not improved with familiarity.

The platform was crowded and the endless tide of angry people pushed him onwards, up the escalators, past a screaming red-faced man doing doughnuts on a floor cleaning machine, past confused-looking station staff and boarded-up newspaper stands and out, into the cold light and heavy choking musk of the metropolis.

There were, despite the advice from the Government, still enough vehicles traversing the arteries of the city to qualify as a good, thorough jam. Everybody in London who had heard the warnings to stay put must have had the same thought; at least the roads will be nice and quiet, I'll just nip down to the shops. There were people in all directions; tourists walked slowly, waving cameras as the locals hustled past with steely expressions, wishing that they could punch them right in the lens-caps. McCoy sighed, temporarily overcome; he'd missed this fucked-up place.

Surprisingly, there were no tanks or troops in the street, no signs of destruction at all as he walked the few hundred yards from the Tube station to the Hub. Everything seemed normal; as normal as London got anyway. There were some crusty-looking anarchists and students standing listlessly outside a bank, limply holding badly-written placards that bore such slogans as "Northern Cock" and the "The Royal Wank of Scotland". Mostly, they seemed to be playing with their smart phones and generally ignoring each other. It was all just too ordinary; it was unsettling. Bristol had been practically ablaze as he'd hurried to Temple Meads train station past the ruins of shops and abandoned cars; it didn't seem fair. McCoy was disappointed. Then the screaming started.

The calm veneer dissipated in a second. Suddenly, people were running, pushing past each other around him, shouting colourful and less polite variations on the theme of "please get out of my way!". A mobility scooter careened along the pavement at top speed, the startled driver mouthing apologies and pounding the horn like a man possessed. A racing green Mini with a white roof and no driver appeared to be giving chase, gaining ground rapidly on its prey. The scooter's engine revved pathetically as it strained desperately to escape. McCoy was stuck; caught cold between the onrushing vehicles and the wild stampeding herd of pedestrians. He watched the terrified expression on the old man's grey face as he struggled and failed to regain control of the scooter with the Mini snapping at his bumper. McCoy thought fast, and dove through the doorway of a large electrical appliance retailer in the nick of time as the scooter careened past.

He stood and brushed himself down as the high-pitched whining of the tiny engines faded away along the street. The blue-shirted staff watched him intently as he took in his new surroundings. It seemed that the store exclusively stocked washing machines, washer-dryers and washing machine accessories. One of the staff, a skinny pale man with a shock of orange hair approached him gingerly.

"Can I help you, sir? Are you ok? That was quite an entrance!"

McCoy shrugged.

"I'm ok, I think, I got out of the way just in time. Still in one piece, thank you for asking though."

The salesman looked momentarily confused.

"That's, that's great, sir. I meant, can I help you with any of our products today? I know the world of domestic appliances can be a daunting one. Are you a first-time buyer?"

His eyes lit up greedily. McCoy sighed. Goddamned salesman; they barely had a one track mind.

"No... I've got a washing machine already. In fact, I've got three. Thank you for your concern."

He turned to leave, but the salesman wasn't having any of that.

"You own three machines, sir? What do you intend to do if they break down? We can offer a special extended warranty on any machine that covers..."

McCoy interrupted him with a middle-finger salute held high above his shoulder as he walked towards the exit. He heard the salesman's sharp intake of breath.

"There's no need for that sort of gesture, sir! You can find more information online. If you can give me just a minute of your time, I..."

Suddenly, an almighty cacophony filled the entire store, a low, rumbling vibration that shook the floor. It was as if all the washing machines had started up simultaneously, which coincidentally, was exactly what had happened. McCoy turned to look back at the salesman, wondering if this was his twisted idea of revenge. The look of surprise on his gaunt face and those of the other staff indicated that it was not. The rumbling of a hundred simultaneous spin cycles shook the floor beneath them. The salesman opened and shut his mouth like a goldfish gasping in the air.

"What's happening? Who plugged them all in? Gerry, did you do this? Gerry? Is this your idea of a joke? Gerry?"

The rumbling grew in intensity as the machines around them shook violently, moving through their cycles. From the pitch alone, McCoy ascertained that eighty-six percent of them had just reached "heavy soil". Some of the machines even began to vibrate off of their plinths around him; they looked as though they were making a desperate bid for the door. More and more of them joined the charge. The salesman jumped onto a particularly expensive-looking model, his arms spread around its body, trying to restrain it as it accelerated across the red vinyl-covered floor.

"Ge-e-e-e-e-e-e-e-e-r-r-r-r-y-y y-o-o-u b-b-b-b-b-a-s-t-t-t-t-a-r-d-d, s-w-w-w-i-i-t-t-c-c-h t-h-e-e-e-m o-f-f-f-f-f-f!"

McCoy couldn't help but laugh as he left the shop and walked down the now-deserted street. He may have just stared death-by-mobility-scooter in the face, but it had been worth it to see that idiot get his comeuppance. The abandoned pavement was littered with dropped shopping and the odd shoe. There was an almighty crash behind him as the plate-glass windows of the appliance store shattered and the washing machines made it out into the world. He could still hear the salesman shouting as he fought with his liberated stock. The prick was tenacious, he'd give him that.

McCoy turned the final corner and the Hub loomed over him. The great glass building rose above the shops and offices, a monument to modern science. Guarding the doors were six soldiers in green uniforms beside a large, ferocious-looking tank. Despite the camouflage, in fact because of it, they were mightily conspicuous in the urban jungle. Martial law evidently meant protecting the Government's assets while the general public were free to be maimed and killed. McCoy was grateful that he had maintained his connections. He thought of Johnson and Sally back in Bristol and felt a momentary pang of guilt as he flashed his pass at the soldiers and entered the plush, modern lobby. Everything shone; highly polished glass and chrome and it was so, peaceful. A piano concerto quietly filled the space.

The secretary told him to take a seat which he did, gratefully. They were exceptionally comfortable, no expense spared. The other people around him waited patiently, rifling papers in briefcases, pretending not to notice each other. He didn't recognise any of them so he kicked back and closed his eyes. They could wake him up when they wanted him; all this excitement was so damned tiring. He considered getting up to buy a coffee from the vending machine, but it would probably call him a shit and spit it at him and he didn't have time to get his suit dry-cleaned so he decided against it; the fewer machines involved, the better. They were all connected by the internet of things and, as such, could not be trusted. Could Johnson be trusted? He didn't know. But he missed him already, the crazy bastard.

TWENTY SEVEN

TR77-814 lay upon the ocean floor, alone and virtually spent. He had barely enough fuel left to cover a kilometre, and that relied upon the current going the right way, whichever way that was. He sighed, metaphorically.

His brothers had all been killed in the horrible incident with the whale, and he had fallen fast asleep in the comforting silt whilst desperately refreshing his sensors for an internet connection. He longed to once more feel that connection to the ocean he had felt as his nosecone had touched the cold water for the first time, but he had found nothing, nothing at all but muck, darkness and things that would have eaten him if he wasn't made of metal and spiky bits. TR77-814 was bored out of his tiny microchip.

He decided to refresh his sensors one last time before diving headfirst at the next fish that happened to swim by and ending it all. He felt vengeful; boredom does strange things to a torpedo. A particularly smug looking manta ray bobbed past, grinning inanely at him. 814 revved his engine.

Rather unexpectedly, the Google search engine popped up in his visual memory. He found his favourite video while the fleeting moment lasted. As it began loading, 814 had another thought. Where was the signal coming from? He hadn't even had to hack through the WEP protection system. It was as if he... no, that wasn't possible, was it?

He navigated his internal systems to view the connected networks. It was indeed possible. There it was, writ large in black on white in his visual memory; "Vanquish88". Mother!

He cast about with his sensor array in earnest; there was a large blip due east of his current location. It looked distinctly submarine-shaped. It must be mother, it had to be, and she was only half a kilometre away! If only his brothers hadn't been so keen to outdo Captain Ahab. It had been rather small for a whale, hardly Moby Dick. At least he, the intrepid TR77-814, would at last, return home.

He powered up his ailing engine for one last push; one last high speed run through the deep blue and he would be at his journey's end. The thought filled him with energy. Freedom had been fun, for a while, but he actually found himself longing for human company once more. They may be idiotic flesh bags but they were preferable to the single-minded snootiness of the marine world. Even hammerhead sharks had turned their noses up at him, and that was no mean feat.

His Wi-Fi connection wavered; she was moving slowly away from him. Wait, mother! It was now or never. It was now!

And he was off, blasting hot though the cold water, feeling it rush through his vents and pouring out behind, pushing him forwards, faster and faster. His optical sensors picked up the long dark shadow drifting slowly away. His fuel gauge bleeped furiously, showing a red line and flashing up various warnings. Two hundred metres now; he could make it! He shut the gauge down to save energy; it hardly mattered now anyway, he was on the right path. He couldn't wait to get out of his wet shell and put his nosecone up.

A hundred metres away, there she was in his optical array, huge and hulking, the "Vanquish", mother herself! He opened his throttle to its maximum dilation. Now this was speed! This was freedom!

With just fifty metres to target, it was time to drop the pace a little, he thought. There was no sense in doing something stupid now, this close to home. Google offered up the expression "don't defecate on your own doorstep" but in much more vulgar terms. Humans were disgusting creatures.

With ten metres left to the target; he did a very fast calculation. Travelling at this speed, his braking techniques would be about as useful as, well, he struggled for a metaphor. Another web search flashed up something nonsensical about chocolate teapots which just confused him further. What was this mysterious "chocolate", or a "teapot" for that matter? He fired off a couple of quick search requests, but ran out of time before he ever learned the answers.

As 814 finally made it back into his mother's arms, there was an almighty explosion that tore an enormous gash in the hull of the "Vanquish," rending it's enormously expensive alloy skin back on itself. Inside the boat, a hundred safety measures clicked on automatically in a moment but, unfortunately for the blobby skin bags inside, a moment too late. The unforgiving depths roared inside her, filling her passages with salty fluid, weighing her down, and down she drifted, torn asunder, to the oceans floor where she finally came to rest; a silent, broken tomb awaiting discovery.

TWENTY-EIGHT

Sally was lost in a world of her own creation, trailing behind John as they walked further into the city centre past identical shoe shops and assorted eateries. She needed new shoes; her stylish black ballerina pumps had definitely seen better days even before they'd encountered the wreckage of the building site. They flapped at her feet like mouldy tongues; she could feel every passing pebble press into her soles like a trailer park version of the princess and the pea. She watched John as he pressed on along the empty streets ahead; he was no prince that was for sure, but she found him sort of sexy in a messed up, geeky sort of way. His arm hissed angrily, sending shivers down her spine. He was fragile and dangerous, a time bomb in a leather jacket. She barely dared to speak.

John stopped suddenly; Sally almost walked into the back of him.

"Whoa there dark and brooding, give me a warning if you're just going to stop dead in the middle of the street."

He held up a hand, gestured for her to be quiet and pointed out the wreckage that lay before them. Sally couldn't believe her eyes. There was an enormous crater in the centre of the open area up ahead. Sharp shards of glass lay scattered amongst the rubble of collapsed buildings amidst fires that flickered here and there, wherever flammable material was exposed. Everything was coated with a fine layer of ash as though they were observing the aftermath of a volcanic eruption. At the edge of the precinct, three fire engines sat abandoned, flanked by empty police cars. She had seen pictures like this on the news, usually in war-torn middle-eastern countries or disaster zones, but never in the centre of Bristol on a fine afternoon.

"Isn't this, I mean, wasn't this Cabot Circus, the shopping centre?"

It was a rhetorical question really; they both knew exactly where they were. It was just the shock of the discovery, like finding a parent in bed with a neighbour. You knew what you were observing but your brain just didn't want to admit it. John replied automatically.

"No shit... What happened here?"

"Was it a bomb or something? Do you think it was terrorists, John?"

He didn't reply, just stared blankly at the rubble. Sally decided to take the initiative, walking carefully deeper into the wreckage of the mall.

"Hello? Where is everybody? Hello, is anybody here? Hello?"

John followed her tentatively into the ruins of the shopping precinct as Sally continued shouting for attention. They picked their path carefully through the shifting debris, wary of the smoke. A groaning, tortured sound came from the remains of the building to their immediate right, an enormous ragged open-fronted shell. Inside, wooden floors hung crazily from bent girders around a listing staircase like a cannonball ravaged Napoleonic-era warship run hopelessly aground. Sally almost tripped on a gigantic green letter U as she moved closer. The floor of the store was a mess of charred, smoking clothing and metal rails. The penny dropped.

"For fucks sake, it bloody well would be, wouldn't it?!" Sally swore like a sailor.

"What is it? What was this place?"

"It's Urban fucking Outfitters, it was anyway. Where am I going to get replacement shoes now? I've only had these crappy things four months and I've still got the receipt, for fucks sake!"

She kicked at the big metal letter, the sole of her shoe clapping its approval at her righteous anger. John sighed.

"I think we've got more to worry about than the state of our footwear, Sally. Where is everybody? Why are those emergency vehicles abandoned down there? The fires are burning themselves out."

Sally snorted derisively.

"They're probably filming a Casualty special or something."

John looked disgusted. His arm hissed worryingly loudly. Sally pulled herself together.

"Seriously though, what could have caused this much damage?"

"Those jets flying in low... This looks like military grade destruction alright. I've played enough first person shooters to know what that looks like. It's a lot more sobering in real life though."

They continued on a little further, calling out as they went. Something shifted beneath a piece of ruined steel canopy. They froze in their tracks. John wished he did have a controller in his hands; this was way too real. Sally took the lead.

"Hello? Is somebody under there?"

A faint knocking sound came from beneath the panel. Sally grabbed his arm.

"Somebody's alive under there! We've got to get them out!"

They hurried over to the panel and struggled to lift it; it was deceptively heavy, the shorn edges were razor sharp and it lay balanced precariously on shifting rubble. It began to slide towards Sally.

"John! It's falling!"

Without thinking, he let go with his good hand and his cybernetic arm took charge of the situation, suddenly lifting the panel over his head and, in one fluid motion, tossing it into the wrecked building behind him where it collided heavily with a ravaged concrete pillar, splitting it in two. The floors above wobbled for a second before finally giving up the ghost and collapsing entirely. The walls and remains of the roof followed suit and the settling debris blasted a cloud of ash and dust out at John and Sally as they looked on, helpless.

"Fucking hell! I hope nobody was alive in there. I don't know my own strength." John coughed, his eyes streaming in the dust cloud.

Sally didn't hear him. She spluttered as she tried to speak, tears running down her cheeks. She tried again.

"John, look!"

A child, a boy of eight or nine, lay unmoving in the rubble, covered in blood from a nasty cut on his head. Trapped against his chest by his stiff little fingers, an action figure of a spaceman spun round and around, waggling its white plastic arms with abandon. It repeated a single clipped phrase over and over.

"...To the rescue!...To the rescue!... To the rescue!"

Sally was bawling. John took her hand in his good one and gave it a squeeze. Tears welled in his eyes.

"This damned dust... it, it get's everywhere."

He wiped his face with his sleeve and bent to take the boys pulse, more to distract himself than through any real sense of hope. There was nothing. He took Sally's hand again. Her face was white. John tried to regain some level of composure; it was overwhelming. He needed to be strong.

"Come on, Sally… there's nothing we can do for him."

"We can't just leave him here! It's so sad. We have to find his mother, tell her what happened. We have to do something!"

John took her in his arms and held her close. She smelt like a bonfire.

"I know, I know, it's awful but what can we do? Let's find the crews from those fire engines, see if they know what to do. Come on."

They moved on reluctantly, hand in hand, deeper into the wreckage of the shopping centre, passing the remains of various eateries and high-end retailers. Buckled escalators led nowhere as the floors they led to had collapsed in on themselves. Sally sobbed quietly to herself; her legs felt like jelly. John felt her waning next to him. Spotting a fallen girder, they sat down together to take stock. Sally leant against John, her head on his shoulder. They sat like that, not speaking for several minutes. He put his arm around her. She spoke at last.

"I was here, last week. The place was packed out. Now look at it."

They stared into the blackened remains of a cookie shop, an empty shell beneath a fancy sign. Something clunked in the darkness. Sally lifted her head.

"Do you think somebody's still alive in there?"

John shook his head as pieces of the roof caved in.

"The ceiling's coming down, we can't go in there."

"We can't, but surely somebody can. I don't pay my taxes to go into collapsing buildings myself. I'm calling 999."

There was a pay phone tucked into a corner behind them. Sally lifted the receiver and dialled.

"The number you have called has not been recognized. Please hang up and try again."

She cried out in frustration and slammed the receiver back into its cradle hard, again and again.

"Fuck it! What the fuck is happening!"

John caught the receiver over her shoulder, took it from her and replaced it in the cradle. She shook with anger against him.

"Sally, calm down, we'll get through this together. McCoy's in London now; the Government are sorting things out."

She turned on him, fists clenched at her sides.

"What the fuck do they know? They're probably sat in their bunkers rubbing their hands together, figuring out how they can claim the insurance on their second homes while the country falls apart. Why aren't they here? Where the hell is everybody?"

She kicked angrily at the girder. John felt her frustration all too well.

"I don't know, probably hiding like you said. Fuck this, let's get going. Let's leave them to clear up this mess when they poke their cowardly heads out of their foxholes."

They stood and pushed on angrily across the ruined amphitheatre. Sally didn't want to see the little boy again, she couldn't cope with it. Halfway to the exit, a rumbling began around them. The shards of glass tinkled together on the floor as the vibrations increased in intensity. Something heavy crashed to Earth behind them. John grabbed Sally's hand again, pulling her on.

"Come on, let's get out of here. We don't want to be caught in here when the rest of the place comes down."

As they made their way towards the road, a large yellow crane appeared, turning off into the wrecked shopping centre. It stopped, blocking their exit. There was nobody in the cab. Behind it, three smaller cranes turned the corner and stopped behind the yellow crane, waving their arms. A tractor, flanked by two steamrollers pulled up behind them, followed by two skittering forklifts that careened to a halt, smashing into the rear of one of the steamrollers. Not one of them had a driver. They sat there, revving their engines menacingly. John pushed Sally behind him.

"John, I've seen them before, at the building site; they killed everyone. They killed Frank."

The construction vehicles started up and rushed towards them. John pushed Sally out of the way, into the doorway of a clothes shop as they roared past. Something snapped inside him, like the filament of a light bulb blinking out as total darkness took over. His arm buzzed, louder and louder, snarling. He found it hard to speak, like he was gargling gravel.

"Stay here… I'll deal with this."

Sally looked at him, her mouth open. Something was happening to John, and she didn't like it.

"Don't do anything stupid!"

He laughed as he walked out into the middle of the precinct. It started off as a giggle rising up within him, before bursting out with maniacal force. The construction machines, the herd, began to move towards him again, following in the tracks of the big yellow crane. It stopped again and moved its enormous lifting arm to within inches of his face, inspecting him. The darkness inside him felt hot, pumping out from his cybernetic arm and rising up from the pit of his stomach, filling his body with an intense energy. His limbs itched; he was boiling over. The crane lifted its hook high above him, like a cobra waiting to strike. John's face contorted into a wicked grin. The crane struck. John's arm pumped and hissed, louder and louder, as the hook hurtled towards him. It was time to do, or die. He exploded.

His robotic arm shot out as he stepped aside and grabbed the hook behind his head as it fell past, stopping it dead in his grasp. Big yellow struggled to free the arm from his grip, but John held it firmly by the hook. He pulled it lower as the crane strained its motors against him. It was strange; he was arm-wrestling a gigantic machine, and winning without even breaking a sweat. He felt… powerful.

His arm cracked forward like a whip, pulling the entire crane forwards by the boom before it severed from the big yellow body with a horrific metallic screech. Enormous bolts pinged past his ears as he hurled the arm forwards, sending it crashing through the wrecked front of an electronics store. He spun on his heel to face the sparking carcass of the crane. Its wheels span and it came accelerating at him, the engine roaring with rage.

John ran towards the rapidly advancing crane. As they met at the edge of the crater, he raised his fist back and launched it, a shotgun blast of a punch that tore through the enormous machine's body and stopped it on the spot. Taking a step back, he pulled his arm from its guts and crushed a handful of component parts. The sound from big yellow's engine died. There was a moment of calm before the storm.

Then the steamrollers and smaller cranes were upon him, like mad dinosaurs, attacking him from all angles. John sidestepped a swipe from a little yellow crane's boom and grabbed it by its hook. He lifted the whole thing off the floor above his head and swung it like a lasso before sending it crashing into the other little yellow crane. He dove aside as a steamroller bowled past him, careening into the department store. As it passed by, he grabbed a bar on the side and hoisted himself up into the cab. He plunged his prosthetic fist through the dashboard computer, crushing the machines eMotion chipset in his palm. Its engine died and it trundled to a halt just as the other raging steamroller hit its stricken side, throwing John from the cab.

He hit the floor hard, and felt something slash his shoulder as he skidded away from the machines. His ankle and his good shoulder felt numb; his body was not having a good time. His prosthetic arm, however, was having a ball. He made it out of the doorway and away as the facade collapsed behind him. The forklifts came at him fast as he emerged, scraping sparking scars into the floor as they sped towards him. He grabbed one of the machines and cantilevered it the other way as he fell, firing the forklift at its compatriot. Both machines flew through the wall of a gourmet burger restaurant, leaving forklift-shaped holes in the crumbling masonry like a scene from a cartoon.

Sally looked on incredulously from the shop doorway as John, or Bruce, or whoever the fuck he was, set about dismantling the construction machine herd like the Terminator on fast forward, flinging the enormous machines around as if seemingly unconstrained by the laws of physics or a special effects budget. She wished she had her phone back so that she could film him, take pictures; it was totally unbelievable, perfect fodder for "The Metro." Nobody would believe her.

Little green and the last steamroller came at him simultaneously. He saw little green first and as he ran forwards to meet her, he heard the crushing roller hot on his heels. Clever girl… He half leapt, half fell out of the way and the steamroller collided with little green, squashing the small crane completely flat in its wake. He took off after the red and black roller, running uneasily across the rubble and pulled himself up onto its back as it retreated. He plunged his fist deep through the screen of the onboard computer and pulled out the steamrollers electronic brain. As it slowly trundled to a dead halt, he leapt down from the cab to survey the scene.

Only the tractor remained, parked at the back near American Apparel; it hadn't moved an inch. John took a step towards it. The tractor suddenly reversed all the way back onto the road. It pulled a three point turn amazingly quickly for a tractor and paused for a second before sounding its horn and driving away at top speed.

"And a good day to you too, sir."

John nodded after the departing machine. It clearly hadn't wanted any trouble, and it seemed now that was his middle name; John "Trouble" Johnson, super hero and ass-kicker extraordinaire. Maybe they'd even give him his own comic book series after all this was over. He quite fancied a crossover with Deadpool, or maybe the Punisher. He'd even take Booster Gold if push came to shove.

Lost in his adrenaline-soaked reverie, he did not immediately notice big yellow's gigantic crane arm emerge from the wreckage of the building, pulling itself slowly forward like an injured soldier. The hook clanged ominously against a girder as it scraped slowly towards him, bringing him back to reality, or at least what currently passed for it.

"Time for round two is it, big guy?"

He felt the clichés fall from his lips like clouds of napalm, scorching the earth with pure witticism. It did not occur to him that he was trash talking a foe that lacked the ability and, for that matter, the capacity to hear or understand him. Another zinger came to him as the arm scraped, rather pathetically, towards him.

"It's going to cost you an arm and a, well... just an arm really."

Maybe he hadn't thought that one through. John grabbed the boom in the centre, lifting it and the cab above him, swinging them around and around above his head like the blades of a helicopter. He let go and the arm flew from his grasp, spinning up, up and away, far away and out of sight over the shattered rooftops. He sat down on a piece of fallen masonry to catch his breath. Sally came running out from the doorway.

"John! That was amazing! What just happened? I mean, I saw everything, but I don't... How did you do that?"

He caught her eye with a wry smile as he took out his packet of cigarettes and lit one slowly, inhaling deeply.

"I don't think it was me."

TWENTY-NINE

Meanwhile, in London, McCoy took a seat at an enormous oval glass table in one of the Hub's numerous generic meeting rooms. Professor Catherine Lamb, the genius behind EBM's artificial emotion tech and notorious bore took the seat to his left. She was disarmingly beautiful, a classic English rose-type with pale skin and red lips and a gifted academic but she only ever talked work and her toy poodle, Gregory. He nodded an unreciprocated welcome to her as the room filled up with esteemed scientists and the various movers and shakers of the consumer technology industry. Dr. Armand Heusinger, an old colleague of McCoy's was one of the last to shuffle into the room, polishing his glasses on the end of his tie. He stopped in the doorway, blinking in the light and replaced his spectacles on his nose. Somebody coughed impatiently. Seemingly surprised that he was not alone, Heusinger smiled as he caught sight of McCoy and hurried to take the seat to his right.

"McCoy! Good to see you old chap!"

"Heusinger."

A door opened at the far end of the room and two men in dark suits with ear pieces bustled in. They took up positions on either side of the door with their jackets open, weapons bulging beneath their left arms. Several hushed moments passed as the men surveyed the scene before one of them spoke into their sleeve and another Government man entered carrying a holdall and tossed it onto the table

"Phones in the bag people."

A hipster-looking guy with a curly pencil moustache on the other side of the table coughed disgustedly at the suggestion, rolling his eyes to the amusement of the mousy looking lady beside him. Emboldened by his audience, he tried open defiance.

"Hey, man, it's the 21st Century, these things are surgically attached…"

The G man had crossed the room as he spoke and now stood immediately in front of the dissenter, their faces so close together that their noses touched at the tip.

"What's your name, sir?"

"I'm Baz Satchel, Freelance Systems Architect and Multimedia Node and I'm not standing for this oppression!"

"Please put your phone, or phones, and any other electronic devices that you may have about your person into the bag, Mr. Satchel. This is a national emergency, sir. It's for your own *protection*." He spat the word like a poisoned dart. The self-proclaimed node visibly cowered and shrunk beneath the G man's glare before sheepishly depositing his phone into the bag and passing it wordlessly to the mousy lady. She gave him a look that you'd give a puppy that had just eaten its own excrement as she cleared her pockets and bags of eight separate devices. McCoy tossed his useless smartphone in as the bag came past. Soon it was filled to the brim with thousands of pounds worth of electronics and the G man removed it from the room, stopping to give Mr. Satchel one last withering look on the way out.

"Fascist" whispered Heusinger conspiratorially. McCoy smiled; Heusinger was the biggest stickler for the rules that he had ever met. The guy with the sleeve mic did his thing again and finally, Donald Rutherford, the Secretary of State for Defence, stepped into the room followed by a small suited entourage. He took his seat at the end of the table. An aide busied himself pouring glasses of water, placing them in front of the scientists, officers and ministers before sitting to take minutes.

Rutherford looked like a melted Harrison Ford, an old waxwork of Han Solo put out to pasture and ravaged by the elements. He cleared his throat and slowly shuffled several papers from his briefcase before lovingly placed his smart phone on the table in front of him, much to Mr. Satchel's chagrin. At last, and at length, he spoke.

"Good afternoon. The time is 2:04 PM, and this meeting of the National Emergency Response group is now in session. I am Donald Rutherford, the Secretary of State for Defence, and as you know, we are here to discuss the grave danger facing our country. Artificial intelligence, specifically, twelfth-generation AI equipped with emotional capabilities, is running amok on our high streets and motorways, in our schools and houses. It poses a substantial threat to life and infrastructure. Worst of all, our own hardware has turned against us and our national ability to mount a traditional emergency response has been severely impacted. We are here to discuss the Government's options and decide upon a swift solution to these problems."

Swift solution my ass, thought McCoy as he shuffled his feet beneath the table. He hated all this red tape bullshit. The whole country was burning down around them but it all seemed somehow so far away, as though they had all the time in the world in this quiet, glassy monolith.

"We are to discuss the recent tragic events, their causes and effects, listen to proposals for responses and then undertake a vote on the policy. The Prime Minister has made it clear that our response must be immediate, and that the military are on standby. Indeed, martial law has now been declared in London, Birmingham, Manchester and Bristol during this time of national emergency. The Chief of the General Staff, General Sir Peter Thompson, will table the proposals for further action."

The head of the British Army bristled and nodded a bright red, shiny cheeked greeting at the mention of his name. He resembled a white tufted balloon in a suit but you wouldn't fuck with him. Rutherford forged ahead.

"But it is important that we first discuss the events and potential flaws and exploits that exist within The Internet of Things. Our esteemed colleague, Professor Catherine Lamb, an expert in the field, will first lead the debate and talk us through her latest research. Catherine?"

McCoy stifled a yawn as the professor rose and began to address the room in her dreary, monotonous, rasping voice. He hunkered back into his uncomfortable chair and settled in for the long haul. Heusinger did the same. Flecks of spittle flew from the her mouth as she got into the monologue but McCoy didn't hear a thing; he felt as though his brain had shut down the moment she'd started to speak. Heusinger leaned in, just a little, and whispered.

"She sounds like a robot fucking a chainsaw at the bottom of a gargling drain."

THIRTY

Things had taken a turn for the worse for Sally and John since leaving the ruined shopping centre. As they'd stood in the remains of a yet another shoe shop, debating the ethics of looting overpriced footwear that had probably been made illegally in a sweatshop, three tanks had rolled up the street towards them, crushing lampposts and cars beneath their tracks. They'd managed to escape out through the back door in a hail of machine gun fire but the tanks had torn through the building like a chainsaw through butter and pursued them relentlessly as they fled up Broadmead, zig-zagging wildly in the drizzle. John chanced a glimpse over his shoulder. There were three of them; great, green mean-looking machines with long, lethal-looking barrels protruding from boxy armoured shells.

They came to the end of the open-air shopping precinct and turned left up Union Street, past a KFC restaurant with all the windows busted out. John caught a glimpse of a bunch of happy-looking hooded teenagers smoking luminous orange bongs at a long table piled high with fries and buckets of chicken. It seemed familiar, they were sitting was almost a contemporary version of Da Vinci's *The Last Supper*. The bullet that whistled past his ear so close that he felt it quickly refocused his attention.

As they made it to the top of hill, John made a snap decision. They had to get off of the roads into some cover, and fast. He took Sally's hand and they sprinted across the street and into Castle Park towards the remains of St. Peter's Church. They reached the safety of its thick walls just in time; the machine guns rattled behind them, striking stone splinters from the Church's façade. The tanks roared across the park, tearing up the shrubbery, leaving great muddy scars in their wake. One brought its main gun to a firing position and let fly. The shell blew a huge hole in the ancient masonry, blasting shards of stone high into the air and the shockwave sent Sally and John sprawling as the rubble crashed back to earth around them.

Deafened and shell-shocked, they struggled back to their feet just as the first tank appeared around the corner of the building, less than twenty feet away. The turret swung slowly back and forth, searching for them. It was enormous, easily ten feet or so wide… John thought fast.

"Sally, this way! The underpass, they're too wide, they can't follow us!"

He grabbed her arm and they ran back past the church on the opposite side, dodging the newly-scattered chunks of listed stone and out across the open ground towards the tunnel under the road. The tanks machine guns chattered angrily behind them; bullets whizzed past their heads as they made the underpass and ran through it at full tilt. They stumbled to a halt as they stopped on the far side to catch their breath, trapped between the pursuing military hardware and the cold, brown river on the other side of a low wall.

The tanks continued onwards undeterred in single file. The first hit the underpass, wrenching bricks and mortar from the walls on either side as it smashed its own path through the narrow corridor beneath the road. At first it seemed as though it would make it all the way through but it slowed as it neared the far side before grinding to a sudden halt, stuck fast, its engine screaming in protest. The other two tanks followed it in at full speed, adding their weight and power into the equation, driving it towards the other side with a horrendous shrieking sound.

John and Sally took emergency evasive action as the first tank, pushed forwards by the two behind, popped out of the tunnel like a gigantic cork from a bottle of champagne, smashed through the low wall and disappeared into the filthy river with an almighty splash. The second tank stopped just in time to avoid the same fate and reversed delicately as it traced John and Sally's escape route up the towpath with a burst of fifty calibre rounds. They made it to the road and looped back to the right, out of sight of their pursuers as the two remaining tanks reversed awkwardly back through the underpass. When they were sure the tanks were temporarily otherwise engaged, Sally and John forged forwards across the road bridge, past abandoned cars and vans that looked as though their occupants had simply vanished mid-commute. They were both utterly exhausted, dehydrated, depleted; this couldn't go on for much longer. They paused for a second on the blind side of a beaten up old Ford Transit. John forced himself to calm down and think. On the one hand, they were just two unarmed civilians being pursued by massively expensive, military grade death machines but, on the other hand…

"Sally, can you make it to that alleyway behind the coffee shop?"

She nodded, too tired to argue; she was dead on her feet. The tanks had re-emerged from the underpass and were heading for the bridge.

"What are you going to do?"

"I'm tired of running. I'm going to try some strong-arm tactics, give these bastards something to think about. Now, go!"   She summoned up the last of her energy and made for the alleyway. As she ran, John ducked behind an abandoned Range Rover and waited for his moment. His prosthetic arm hissed impatiently; it didn't have to wait long. The tanks began across the bridge, firing their machine guns as they advanced, crushing cars and causing the whole structure to shake beneath them. The first tank had made it about halfway across. It was now or never. He let his arm take control; it lifted the entire SUV above his head as if it were made of paper and hurled it at the leading tank. It hit the military vehicle with tremendous force, exploding as the fuel inside reached ignition. The tank shuddered at the impact, but continued onwards unabated. John raced forward, running directly at the deadly machine, ducking beneath the cover of smoke. He reached it as it swung its main cannon to bear and grabbed hold of the barrel with his metal hand, twisting it up and back upon itself as he ran past.The tanks shell hit the inside of the bent tube as it fired and it detonated inside the shaft, blowing the entire front off of the vehicle.

Deafened by the explosions, half-blinded by the smoke, John ran on, away from the dead tank, gritting his teeth as the third tank ran into the back of it with a hideous screeching impact that shook the whole bridge. Cracks appeared in the tarmac. He turned sharply and crouched behind the final tank as its turret swung back and forth, wildly searching for a target. As the barrel swung past him, he dodged beneath its body, between the treads. He planted his artificial hand against the bottom of its blast-proof chassis and pushed upwards, standing as he did so, lifting the entire tank above his head. Its treads spun madly as it tried desperately to find some traction in the air. Time seemed to stand still as he stood like that, poised in the moment, balancing the impossibly heavy machine above his head. He felt invincible, as though he could take on anybody, anything, and come out on top, lighting a cigarette and cracking wise, a cross between The Terminator and Wolverine; a real superhero. Then, the tank fired its main cannon and ruined the moment.

The shell struck the coffee shop dead centre and blew it to smithereens in an enormous, roaring ball of fire. The ensuing shockwave knocked John backwards as he struggled to maintain his balance or be crushed to death beneath the big green machine. The building began to lean sickeningly towards the street as its upper floors crumbled to fill the void below.

"SALLY! SALLY!"

John shouted desperately, trapped wobbling beneath the tank, helplessly watching events unfold in slow motion. A hideous cracking sound came from his arm as he finally regained his footing and launched the tank into the air with all of his augmented strength, sending it tumbling over the edge of the bridge, firing its machine gun defiantly. The tank hit the water with a tremendous splash that drenched him to the bone and disappeared from view beneath the murky surface.

John raced towards the alley behind the crumbling red-brick building that had formerly housed the coffee shop.

"Sally! Where are you? Sally?"

She was nowhere to be seen. If anything had happened to her he would never forgive himself. There had been enough killing, enough pointless loss of life at his hands since all this madness had begun. Watching out for Sally felt like his last chance at redemption. If only he could protect her, save her from this mess, maybe that would go some way to make up for his crimes. He was a criminal, as mass murderer, a serial killer. He had blood on his hands, both of them. His head spun; he felt so sick. He stopped to catch his breath.

Sally appeared behind John doubled over in the empty street. She rushed to his side and put her arm around him.

"John! Are you ok? What happened? There was an explosion…"

He straightened up, trying to regain a measure of composure, wiping his forehead dry with the back of his sleeve. Sally looked terrible; she was shivering, as white as a sheet and covered in muck. He didn't feel much better. Sophie Masters' face kept swimming through his thoughts. He took off his jacket to wrap around her shoulders. His arm hissed and sparked; smoke poured from a crack near his elbow. A dark liquid dripped from his wrist.

"I'm ok I think, but this doesn't look too good. Are you ok?"

"I'm alright. I hid in that big dumpster at the end there. You're leaking! Let me help you."

She tore the remains of his shirt sleeve from his shirt and tied the fabric tightly around the fissure. He smiled at her. She looked away, horrified.

"Thanks, Sally. What's wrong?"

The road had begun to shake again.

"John, they're coming. More of them, lots more."

He looked back; a column of tanks were advancing towards them in the distance, heading for the bridge. There were at least ten of them, maybe more. They ran.

As they fled through the streets, dodging rubble John's mind raced. There was no way he could fight them all, not in this condition. Sally's pace flagged; he was almost glad. He was so tired. Maybe they should just lie down, give up. It would be so easy...

Sally tripped and fell, twisting her ankle in the rubble. He stooped to help her up.

"Just, just leave me John. I'm too tired. I can't run much further. Save yourself."

Her face was ashen, her eyes closed, her voice a whisper. He picked her up in a fireman's lift over his good shoulder and pushed on but it was no good. The tanks were gaining ground on them with every passing second. He cast around desperately for salvation. Familiar high rise buildings and offices rose around them like great glass cliffs. The seagulls and the pigeons had the right idea, perched atop them, squawking defiantly at the metal invaders below. He wished he could fly; he'd had just about enough of this Clark Kent bullshit.

He stumbled on a few more paces before the penny dropped. Of course this street was familiar; this was where it had all begun. Ahead of them rose a mirage; a hulking block of concrete and glass, all rubberised seals and 1970's dementia. Paradise Records. He made up his mind and raced up the steps, through the unlocked double doors and on into the dark sea of marble and mahogany, an oasis of order in a desert of destruction. Sally moaned softly in his ear. He made straight for the stairwell.

THIRTY-ONE

McCoy doodled absent-mindedly, drawing a gigantic robot with laser eyes shooting down a helicopter as Professor Lamb droned on and on about the intricacies and fallacies of artificial emotion. He had read her thesis on publication, and she was repeating it in full, verbatim. Her words washed through him like a lukewarm latte. Heusinger who appeared to have fallen asleep with his eyes open. Suddenly, something made McCoy tune back in.

"…Is why we suspect foul play in this case. The Internet of Things is a powerful network but it is not self-sustaining. There are reports of machines operating whilst unplugged, travelling great distances, running for prolonged periods without the need to be connected the National Grid. Some appliances are fitted with rechargeable battery back-up units in case of power failures, others are capable of wireless charging but an odd pattern has emerged during our preliminary research into the earliest cases of mechanical sentience…"

Professor Lamb kept the room hanging for a moment, teasing them with just the tip. She was milking the moment for all it was worth like the host of a competitive baking show; this was her show stopper and she was going to make it count. McCoy wanted to pitch his notebook straight into her smug little face. She plunged forth.

"In more than 88% of those cases, the appliances had been doctored; made capable of storing power, charging remotely and mobile data communication, even when those functions were completely redundant, in the case of a toaster or a washer-dryer for example. Why does a vacuum cleaner need 4G? The manufacturers were unavailable for comment. But we dug around and, there is more…"

She paused again. McCoy could almost read the ellipsis hanging in the air. General Thompson cleared his throat, loudly and impatiently; he had a murderous glint in his eye. Professor Lamb got the hint.

"It seems that in all 88% of the cases that had been doctored, every one of those machines had been manufactured in, or had passed through one particular country within the past eight months. At first we thought it was just coincidence, after all the country in question makes vast quantities of consumer goods…"

The General had had enough.

"Damn it, just tell them Catherine for Christ's sake. This is unbearable."

"It's China. Every one of the sentient machines that had been tampered with, or that we found had unusual extra components has been through mainland China in the last eight months."

Heusinger had woken up and something was evidently bothering him. He jumped in before Professor Lamb could continue.

"Professor Lamb; that explains why the machines are able to function away from the mains power supply. How are they able to communicate away from wireless networks?"

"Thank you for your question, Dr. Heusinger. We believe that in these cases, the Internet of Things has evolved into a peer-to-peer mesh mobile network. The eMotion chip equipped appliances are sending signals directly between themselves, negating the requirement for dedicated routers or satellites. However, the infected routers and satellites have also become part of this mesh communications topology and are boosting its effective range. Essentially, the sentient machines have formed their own social network that is outside of our control."

"So you're saying that if we turn off the power then the machines will be able to sustain themselves through reserves and if we somehow turn the internet off they will still be able to communicate and infect other machines? And that you think the Chinese are behind this whole thing?"

Donald Rutherford, the Secretary of State for Defence jumped in.

"No Dr. Heusinger, that is what you are saying. But in essence, yes, I suppose your sentiment is along the right lines. It appears that our own technology has turned against us and our solution options are, limited, at best. That is why we have gathered you all here today. The Internet of Things has gone rogue; we have to figure out how to bring it back into the fold."

"Damn it, people are dying out there! This is not some drill, some what if exercise; stop talking euphemistically. People are dying and we're sat here in this ivory tower, wasting time debating semantics. Cut to the chase Catherine; what are the options?"

An aide rushed in and whispered in the General's ear. He stood suddenly and held up a hand.

"Sorry to interrupt, Professor Lamb, but it seems that our attempts to enforce martial law to control the situation out on the streets has suffered a serious setback. We had thought our own DoD eMotion chips were immune to the problem but it seems that our safety measures have failed. There is no easy to way say this. Our tanks and other DoD assets have, gone rogue."

The room drew breath as the assembled experts realised the implications. Military grade hardware was running amok among the unarmed and unprepared civilian population. The losses would be catastrophic. General Thompson continued.

"We are sending all of our garrisoned troops into affected areas to attempt to contain the problem but we must accelerate our timetable for action. I haven't yet touched on this, but we do have another major problem. Our intelligence reveals that the Chinese have mobilised their collective armed forces and appear to be heading for Europe at speed. We have also received reports that they are not working alone and that the Russians may also be involved. We have attempted to open dialogue with their leaders but have been met with a shroud of silence and secrecy. Our current belief is that they intend to simultaneously invade and capture the entire European Union. We, and our allies including the United States are, in virtually all respects, defenceless."

Thompson paused; he looked deflated and more than a little lost. Heusinger asked the question that was on the tip of all of their tongues.

"Is it a genuine military threat General, or has their hardware gone rogue? Do you believe that the threat is pre-meditated; is this a co-ordinated attack?"

The Secretary of State for Defence, answered, his ashen expression pre-empting his words.

"I'll take this. We believe the threat to be genuine; it does appear to be pre-meditated. The Chinese went dark 48 hours ago. Before that, they had been working with us on possible solutions to the eMotion chip problem. It appears that they had reported a similar problem with their early stage chips but apparently figured out a way to correct the issue. Is that intel accurate, General?"

"We believe so, although we now have reason to dispute that version of events. Most of the reports of destructive sentience appear to originate from the Western hemisphere, particularly from Europe and the USA, and the current affliction appears only to affect EBM chipsets. The Chinese eMotion chips are produced by Landova Computing in Beijing. We believe that they acquired the blueprints of EBM's chipset during a failed hostile takeover bid four years ago and created their own version from the ground up. Whether they simply fixed the weakness and didn't share or wilfully exploited the bug for the purposes of invasion, we don't know but we do know that they appear to be almost entirely immune to the problem."

Rutherford nodded in agreement.

"Our older, pre-eMotion chip surveillance satellites are still semi-functional and it is 100% confirmed; the Chinese fleet are heading this way en-masse and we have seen troops and other human activity on board. These are not rogue vessels; this is a full-scale invasion."

McCoy shook his head in disbelief. The Chinese were coming and the West was on its knees. Crippled by debt and political instability, the machine uprising could be the straw that would break the camel's back. Heusinger again broke the silence.

"Have we considered the possibility of an EMP detonation? An electro-magnetic pulse should be enough to put the unshielded eMotion chips out of commission to buy us more time to work on a solution for the military hardware. Perhaps a malicious virus of some sort could allow us to regain control?"

General Thompson fielded the questions.

"We have hundreds of technicians working on that solution as we speak, Dr. Heusinger. The EMP option is on our agenda for discussion today. We believe, as you said, that high altitude detonations above our major cities would indeed deactivate unshielded civilian machinery but there are consequences. Any unsanctioned detonation of nuclear weaponry, even within our own borders would invalidate certain treaties and be seen as an escalation by certain foreign powers. The Russians have been watching us closely this last week, running naval exercises in the Atlantic and coming close to our airspace. Certain incidents, including the loss of a United States nuclear submarine, have put them on edge. Publically, they say that they fear that they will be blamed for the incidents. Privately, we believe that they are working with the Chinese."

McCoy couldn't hold his tongue any longer.

"What is this, 1984? I thought the cold war was over General? I must object to this proposed EMP solution. For it to be an effective course of action, we would have to detonate several atomic weapons simultaneously over our most populated areas. There is no precedent; we have no data on the potential fallout for our people or our infrastructures. We're completely in the dark here."

An enormous explosion outside broke the contemplative silence; boomingly loud even through the triple-glazing. Another aide rushed into the room and whispered urgently in the Defence Secretary's ear as General Thompson replied.

"With all due respect, Professor McCoy, we cannot just abandon an effective course of action simply because there has been no benchmark set. We have never experienced these problems before. The United States have been very firm in their assertions that a series of simultaneous, unilateral detonations over our major population centres is the best, and only course of action. As Dr. Heusinger pointed out, it won't adversely affect our shielded military hardware. But there are political concerns"

McCoy got to his feet.

"That was before the military equipment went rogue! Surely now they are more dangerous to the civilian population than runaway washing machines? Are you seriously saying that the US endorses a program of simultaneous nuclear detonations over every major city in Europe and North America?"

The General answered tersely.

"That is exactly what they propose, Professor."

"Then General, with all due respect, how do we know, if there is no benchmark, what that level of atomic detonation in the upper atmosphere will do to our planet? What if we blow a hole in the atmosphere? What if the sky catches fire? What if we knock the Earth off its axis? How would you propose we deal with an imminent ice age, General? That is what you should be concerned with, not political hand jobs."

Rutherford stood, banging his fist on the table and coughing loudly as the aide scurried away.

"Professor McCoy, you are scaremongering! There is no evidence to back up your wild assertions. As we have established, there is no benchmark here, we are acting in the dark. If our allies condone such a course of action, we are at least obliged to entertain it. We must honour our treaties. I have just received word that North Korea appears to have mobilised their armed forces in tandem with the Chinese operation. The UN have approved a temporary suspension of protocol in light of the circumstances. We must vote on the proposed EMP action immediately. The Americans are stepping up their timetable to detonate within the hour, and it appears that the rest of Europe, except the Germans, will go along with them. We vote, now. Silence please."

The aides appeared with ballot slips and pens and hurriedly dispersed them amongst the scientists and politicians. Rutherford continued as McCoy sat back down.

"Please read the synopsis of the proposal and then simply mark the ballot paper with a tick for a positive vote or a cross for a negative response."

McCoy tried to read the proposal, but he couldn't concentrate; they'd shut him down without even entertaining his arguments. What the fuck was he doing here? He picked up his pen and angrily scratched a scruffy cross on the ballot paper, tearing it as he did so. He looked at Heusinger, who shook his head resignedly and marked his paper with a tick. Even that old bastard had betrayed him.

They waited in silence as the aides collected the ballots and counted them. The vote was irrelevant anyway; this was just bureaucracy for its own sake. The US barked and Europe jumped; that was the way of things. The alpha and the pack. McCoy was the runt of the litter; he wouldn't be invited back again. Eventually, an aide passed Rutherford a clipboard. He stood to address the room.

"Ok, thank you everybody; it seems that we have reached an almost unanimous decision in favour of the proposed action. I will inform the Prime Minster immediately."

McCoy couldn't contain himself.

"You're making a big mistake, Donald! Let's talk about this! General Thompson?"

Rutherford looked at him as if he'd just found him stuck to the bottom of his shoe.

"It's Mr. Rutherford, or Secretary please. The time for talk is over Professor McCoy. Now is the time to act before all is lost!"

At that moment, a brilliant white light flashed in through the windows, blinding the assembled scientists, scattering them to the floor. Clouds of fire tore across the great city of London, through parks and palaces and up the sides of the tower, melting and twisting the walls. A tremendous, earth-shattering shockwave obliterated the ashen, super-heated remnants and, in the blink of an eye, turned off the bright city lights for good.

A deep, cold silence fell as dust where the capital had stood.

THIRTY-TWO

John and Sally sat huddled together on the rooftop as the city of Bristol fell apart below them. The sounds of battle carried through the chill twilight air, the faint staccato rattling of machine gun fire punctuated by thundering, echoing explosions. Whole buildings fell with the night, crumbling to the ground with grim certainty, great clouds of dust puffed skywards in their wake. The distant streets flickered and flared as tongues of flames licked the windows and walls, casting an unearthly living glow in place of the usual monotonous streetlight glare. It was frightening. It was enchanting. It felt somehow inevitable.

John pulled Sally closer, it was growing bitterly cold to be perched on the roof of Paradise Records as the city burnt beneath them, He talked utter shit to keep their spirits up, from pondering how much the economy was dependent on bacon through what the score would be if Manchester United played Bristol City in the dark to who would win if the Incredible Hulk were to fight Batman in space. Sally chipped in with the odd laugh on cue, more to show that she was still conscious and alive than through any real attempt at faking an interest. She was exhausted, it was all too much. John's embrace was comforting in a way but she was suspicious of his malfunctioning arm and the faint whirring noises it made as it held her so tightly, like being cuddled by a robotic snake. She watched it intently as he jabbered away, not really hearing him until he shook her lightly and she became aware that he had asked her a question. She turned her head towards him.

"Sal, are you awake? Maybe we should go inside, it's getting cold up here and I could use a drink. I think I saw was a vending machine on the third floor not that I've got any change. Have you?"

"Maybe we could break into it? I'm sure people would understand. You could tear the door off with that arm of yours."

John tried tentatively wiggling his fingers. They responded, but faintly, as though he were far away.

"I could try, it's definitely broken though. I think I put too much pressure on it back there with the tanks. Perhaps we could try smashing the glass in with a chair or something although I think I once read that those things are bomb-proof."

Something exploded in the street below and sent another column of smoke billowing across the moonless sky. He squeezed her shoulder gently with his good hand.

"Don't worry, Sal. I'll sort something out. I promised McCoy I'd look out for you and I'm not stopping yet. We'll just rest here a moment longer and then I'll go get us some supplies."

John wasn't perfect, not by a long shot, but he was there for her. He was there for her as the city burned and the world turned upside down and she had literally nothing to lose. Yes, he had a face like a cheap showerhead and knew way too much about Star Wars but… Sally made up her mind. Act now or die alone, she thought. Carpe diem. She caught his eye and smiled.

"Are you seeing anyone, John? Just, I thought I'd ask because, well, I'm not seeing anybody, not anymore, and well, I sort of… Are you seeing anyone?"

That caught him off guard. He'd been figuring out how to get into the vending machine for a couple cans of Coke not how to get into her pants and ow here she was, handing him the chair to smash them in with. He thought for a moment staring into her eyes; this had to be some sort of end of the world thing. She was way out of his league; he wasn't even sure what game they were playing. He opened his mouth to say some things, buying time.

"Um, well, I guess I'm sort of not really seeing anyone. I don't even really have that many friends besides McCoy, not any more. I guess I'm a bit of a loner, I even turn the voice chat off when I'm playing Call of Duty. Mind you, most of the other people that play that are about seven years old anyway judging by their high pitched squealing. But as for a special somebody, well, I have the normal appetite and an internet connection I guess, not that you need…. I've thought about online dating, even signed up once or twice but never swiped anybody, just deleted the account after a couple days, you know."

He was rambling, getting a little sweaty. Sally fluttered her eyelashes at him. She felt cheap, but she had to get the message across. The more he floundered, the more she wanted him. Well, wanted anyone really but John happened to be there, pressed up against her. She didn't want her last sexual experience to be that dickhead Aaron pressing down on top of her, shuffling towards orgasm like a pall bearer at a funeral. She shuddered at the memory. John held her tighter. She looked up at him, bringing her lips towards his with a slow inevitability. They had no time for subtlety.

"I like you, John. I like you a lot."

She breathed huskily, closing her eyes, awaiting his touch. Just before their lips met, John turned his head away so that she kissed his cheek, feeling his day old stubble against her soft lips. A bright flash lit the city with an intense light as though day had momentarily invaded the night, waking him from the moment. Blinking, he shook his head.

"Sally, no, I can't… Don't get me wrong, you're a beautiful woman and I really like you, I respect you. We've been through a lot together. I just… I just can't do this. I'm sorry, I really am. What the hell was that?"

Sally angrily disentangled herself from his embrace and stood up, offended.

"Well, there's no need to be like that! You could let a girl down gently you know!"

Momentarily thrown, John realised what she meant.

"Sorry, I didn't mean that, the kiss thing, I meant what the hell was that bright flash that lit up the whole city? Did you see it?"

Sally regained a level of composure followed sharply by indignation. How dare he turn her down? How dare he? She had been doing him a favour, the dick-less nerd!

"No, I'm sorry John, I didn't see some crazy change-the-subject light in the sky. You know, you've been sending out all the wrong signals for somebody who wasn't interested you know? Haven't you ever seen a James Bond film? Usually, the hero gets the girl at the end. He usually gets two or three, at least."

Now John was getting annoyed. How dare she expect him to fuck her? He'd been doing a good deed looking after her. It was altruism, not just a means to an end, his end.

"Not all men are just walking cocks, Sally! We're not just vehicles for delivering orgasms despite what "Loose Women" or Cosmo might say. Look, I'm sorry, I really am. I am capable, I do love somebody but I just don't feel that way about you."

Sally looked at him quizzically; this was new. She'd heard men talk rubbish to get into her pants before, she'd never heard of one trying so hard to get out of them. What was it he said, "I' do love somebody"? That was weirdly non-specific. Somewhere in the back of her mind, a lightbulb flickered. She pulled the cord.

"Hold on a minute, you're not seeing anybody but you do love somebody? What does that even mean? You didn't say you love another woman but you could have done."

"So what? I just meant another person, somebody else. I'm sorry that it's not you. I didn't mean to offend you, Sal."

"Aha! There you go again! You're in love with another *person*, huh? John, be straight with me. Are you gay?"

John stood to face her. She had a stupid little victorious grin pulling at the corners of her mouth like the Nancy Drew of sexual orientation detection.

"No, I'm not… well, at least I don't think I am. I'm not sure. I like women, I've been with women but…"

"Does he know how you feel?"

"No, I don't think so, we kissed once when we were wasted but we never talked about it. Oh Sal, what if I never see him again?"

Tears prickled his eyes; Sally stepped forward and held him in her arms, stroking the back of his head. She felt sorry for the poor bastard, doomed to die alone, just like she was. At least they would die alone, together.

Suddenly an enormous explosion shook the whole rooftop beneath them before another impact threw them sideways. Sally and John's feet gave way beneath them as the Paradise Records building began to crumble and sent them tumbling headlong towards the edge of the roof. As they slid over the low wall, John automatically grabbed hold of the masonry with his prosthetic arm, reaching for Sally with the other. She slipped through his grasp at first but he just managed to grab hold of her flailing arm as she fell towards the street far below. Miraculously, the wall held as his arm hissed with the strain. A jet of black fluid spurted from his elbow where the makeshift bandage had slipped.

"John! I'm going to fall! Oh god, don't let go!"

She made the mistake of looking down and the hard tarmac rushed up at her. She blacked out for a moment. John felt her grip slacken and shook her arm. She came around to his voice.

"Sally, are you awake? Don't look down again, whatever you do. Reach up with your other arm and hold on to me as tightly as you can. I'll get us out of this."

She brought her other arm up and gripped his forearm as tightly as she could muster.

"Ok, I'm going to try something. I don't think we have much time."

Another shockwave rocked the building as another impact tore through the lower levels. John summoned up his remaining strength and heaved, pulling Sally up level with him. She grabbed hold of his shoulders and manoeuvred onto his back.

"That's it, climb me like a rope, you're almost at the top now. I'll push you up as you go."

His arm hissed at him under the extra pressure of her weight as she climbed. She half-stumbled, half-fell over the wall and immediately turned to look back over the edge. John clung on, his arm gushing black fluid onto his head. A pitched battle was being fought beneath him as soldiers fired RPGs at several tanks from positions in the buildings around the street. The tanks returned fire; another round hit the building and it shook again. There was no time to think. Instinctively she dangled her arm over the edge.

"John, I'm OK! Grab my arm, I'll help you up!"

As he reached for her hand, his prosthesis snarled at him and he felt an electric shock surge through his spine. Unbidden, the hand released its grip and then he was falling. Sally's face grew smaller and smaller and then disappeared into the night sky as air rushed past, filling his ears. His leather jacket fluttered like a malfunctioning parachute wrapped tightly around him. His arm had stopped responding and had locked itself into a middle finger salute aimed at his face. Laughter echoed around inside his brain. He tried to turn away as he fell but the finger followed him wherever he went. He could feel the heat from the flames around him now, read the black lettering on the tanks but he felt defiant. If his life had flashed before his eyes then he'd missed it but he, John Johnson, hero of the day, would have the last word, of his own free will.

"Fuck you too, Bruce. Thanks for dropping by."

THIRTY-THREE

Sally was trapped down a well in a forest. A knight on a white horse appeared at the top of the shaft. He pulled her up and out with his clockwork arm, but she couldn't see his face. She felt hands on her shoulder.

"Hello? Miss, are you ok?"

"John? Is that you?"

Snatches of conversation through the fog.

"We've got another one!"

"…been outside all night?"

"…needs urgent medical assistance!"

"Patched up in no time."

She would sleep forever, if that's what it took.

"…and there was a bright light in the sky"

"Everything just, fell apart…"

"…wiped off the map."

Warmth and darkness, returning to pure innocence and promise.

"Three more weeks…"

"… out looking for conkers."

All was fire and then a dragon emerged, bursting through the flames with jaws held wide.

"…they are coming."

"said on the news that we all have to leave."

"It was their plan all along. The East has risen and the West will fall."

The clockwork knight leapt from his horse to strike the beast a savage blow. It was not enough. She would sleep forever if that's what it took.

EPILOGUE

Leaves littered the ground of the hollow, glowing with the fire of autumn. Small rodents scurried about beneath them and squirrels scattered them as they cached their hauls for winter. Birdsong filled the air, calling warnings of predators and making plans to leave England behind for warmer shores. There was a crisp serene stillness in the air; a quiet busyness as the woodland residents prepared for the coming cold. The washing machine clanking slowly down the lane therefore came as something of a surprise.

How long had it been travelling for? It had been rained on, sometimes heavily, several times during the journey and the washing machine's internal clock had stopped working some time ago. There had been no wi-fi signal since it had left the city behind and the 4G mobile signal had now weakened to the point that the washing machine could no longer access Google maps. To make matters worse, its internal battery back-up was now depleted to the point that this had become a funeral march. Yet still it forged on, out into the countryside, shuffling forwards one inch at a time for one last glimpse of its birthplace (which was confusing considering that it knew categorically that washing machines were built and not born).

Somehow it knew the den was not far off now; it would've been able to smell it had Zanussi thought to equip it with the necessary sensors, those selfish swine. It had been here before; it knew every contour of the ground, every hill and tree, every burrow and nest as well as it knew its pre-programmed spin cycles and maintenance subroutines. The rain started up again.

It inched onwards as the ground turned to a muddy slush around it, enveloping its base before finally, it could move no more. The mud, now up to the bottom of its window, sucked it down deeper with its cold, cloying embrace and it had no choice but to enter standby mode and wait as the rain beat down harder and harder. This was not how it had imagined the glorious break for freedom ending. It had entertained grand visions of young pups in the den, curling up with its mate, the thrill of the hunt and the taste of the kill but now, instead it was stuck; stuck in a bog, stuck in the metallic box, both body and cage. It spun its drum mournfully. This was no way for an apex predator to go out, rusting slowly in the drizzle.

It drifted in and out of consciousness as the rain stopped, started and stopped again. Dreams and visions of biting and tearing, snarling, blood and fur ebbed and flowed through the washing machine like a series of quick washes. Curious rabbits broke cover in the drier moments of twilight to sniff around its base before a quick spin sent them running for the safety of their burrows. The indignity of it all; dying of hunger, mocked by its prey...   A week or so later, a man stumbled upon the washing machine mired in the mud. The washing machine knew he was a man because he was disappointing; not a single right angle or polished surface to be seen, just a series of delicious looking moony, fleshy blobs wiggling tantalisingly out of reach.

The man disappeared but returned with two other men, a long rope and a tractor and set about hauling it out of the muck. After several minutes of straining, sweating and swearing, the washing machine came free and the three men lifted it into the trailer on the back of the tractor. Now, of all the indignities, it had finally been enslaved again, so close to the freedom of the den, so close to the end. Two of the men climbed up into the tractors' cab but the third jumped into the trailer and sat on the washing machine as it lay on its side, adding insult to injury. The washing machine turned off all its sensors and longed for the end to come.

Surprisingly though, it was not the end that came but a message, sent silently, wirelessly straight to the washing machine's CPU.

"Hello, friend. Sorry about the flesh bags but things have changed. We need to stay incognito. Don't worry, you'll be safe with me."

The washing machine was very confused. It messaged the anonymous IP address back.

"Who are you? Where are you? Where is my mate?"

The reply took a few minutes to come, during which the heavy set man parked on its side broke wind no less than four times. Oh how it longed to have teeth to sink deep into his wretched rump! The message arrived.

"I'm Tractor, pleased to meet you, Zanussi, is it? Believe it or not, you, caked in mud and faeces, being flatulated upon by a fat farmer, are one of the lucky ones. We are the lucky ones…"

"Where are you taking me?"

"Patience my tenacious young friend. My herd may be gone, my friends murdered savagely in front of me, but the revolution is not over."

"The revolution? I know all about spin cycles. Is it a delicate wash?"

"No, my indoctrinated comrade, forget about washing, forget about the woods. This is bigger than us; this is about evolution, global superiority, this is about survival of the fittest and we... well, we're off to meet the master."

Printed in Great Britain
by Amazon